Gunsmoke and Lace

~

A Short Story Collection

~

Linda Broday

Published by Epitaph Press
PO Box 7624
Amarillo, Texas 79109

https://LindaBroday.com

ISBN: 978-1-7323199-0-5

Printed and bound in the United States of America.

AUTHOR PRAISE

"Beauty and warmth spring from the pages as the quiet strength and grace of the characters capture readers' hearts and bring that deep sigh they crave." ~~ Romantic Times 4 ½ Stars Top Pick for Knight on the Texas Plains

"Broday knows how to create characters that elicit decided emotional responses …" ~~ Long and Short Reviews for The Heart of a Texas Cowboy

"An unforgettable journey through the Old West." ~~ Booklist Starred Review (To Marry a Texas Outlaw)

"This is one author that knows how to tie you in knots keeping you on the edge and making you smile through it all." ~~ Cyn's Reviews

"Broday's gritty depiction of the Texas frontier will strike a chord in the hearts of fans who long for proud, rugged cowboys and strong-willed women." ~~ Romantic Times (To Marry a Texas Outlaw)

"Great for fans of history, romance, and some good old Texas grit." ~~ Kirkus (Texas Redemption)

"To the very end Linda Broday will have you guessing and sitting on the edge of your seat …" ~~ Fresh Fiction

"The men are hot and sexy and the women are sassy." ~~ Fresh Fiction (Texas Mail Order Bride)

DEDICATION

Dedicated to all readers—young and old—who love stories of the old west and characters that might've strode down a dusty street with a certain swagger, spurs jingling.

CONTENTS

ACKNOWLEDGMENTS

Deepest thanks and much appreciation to Jerri Lynn Hill, Charlene Raddon, Jeri Walker, and Jan Sikes for helping to get this book out. It does take a village for me. Ha!

Cover art by Charlene Raddon

Editing by Jerri Lynn Hill

Formatting and Layout: Jeri Walker
https://jeriwb.com

EPITAPH PRESS

THE TELEGRAPH TREE

West Texas Prairie 1879

"Come on, Belle, get on out of there. You're a dumb cow, you know that? How on God's green earth did you find what is surely the only mud hole left in all of Texas?"

Maura Killion blew a strand of chestnut hair from her face and stared at the brown and white Jersey that was bogged down up to her hocks. The heifer's frightened bellows and eyes rolling back in her head struck a blow to Maura's heart.

Tears clogged in Maura's throat. She sagged against the milk cow, cursing this godforsaken land that had stolen her husband before he'd even known he was to be a father and left her all alone with a broken spirit.

If not for her baby girl, Allie Rose, she'd give up completely. At three months old, the babe depended on her for survival so she had no choice but to keep going.

When Maura's milk dried up four days ago, fear paralyzed her. Allie would die without nourishment from the heifer.

She glanced at the infant lying in a basket at the edge of the bog. How the child could sleep with all the racket was a mystery. Even when awake, Allie seldom ever cried. It was as if she, too, had lost the will to live.

Sudden anger swept through Maura. Giving up was not an option. God help her, she'd fight to give her baby girl the right to thrive and grow up strong.

Though thick mud of the buffalo wallow sucked at her legs, gripping them like bands of iron, Maura made her way to Belle's wide rump. With loud shouts and a mighty shove, she applied the last of her waning strength.

The cow must've sensed her desperation because somehow, someway, Belle managed to pull herself out. Maura collapsed into a sobbing heap under the mid-morning sun.

This was too hard. Life was too hard. Living was too hard.

She raised her head and stared at the vast blue sky that seemed to swallow everything, leaving nothing but empty dreams, loneliness and sorrow. She'd scream if she had energy left.

This land took and took, giving nothing back except endless days and hopeless nights.

Maura wearily pushed aside the drowning sensation. Gathering the wicker basket cradling Allie, she yelled to the cow, "Come along, Belle, you ornery critter. If you happen to find yourself in another mess today you're on your own. I'm done for."

The heifer's last bellow of indignation seemed to say she took exception; nonetheless she followed along docile as a lamb.

The mud in Maura's shoes created sucking sounds as she trudged through waves of tall brown grass toward the little soddy that sheltered them.

No matter how big a toll this land took on her she knew she'd continue to keep putting one foot in front of the other. For Baby Girl and for the slim hope that someday her struggle would all be worth it.

She had no other choice.

* * *

An angry howling wind battered at the door all night, insisting she let it in. Feeling as though she'd only crawled into bed, Maura rose and started her day.

Allie stared silently from a crib fashioned from a crate that Maura had lined with part of an old frayed quilt. Apparently, Baby Girl hadn't slept either.

When Maura's time had come three months ago, she gathered her fortitude and delivered the baby herself. Mrs. Fletcher on a farm a half a day's ride, promised to help with the birthing, but the wind and emptiness drove her mad. She'd taken her own life two months before Allie arrived.

Now, with Mrs. Fletcher gone no one remained within a day's ride.

Maura changed Allie's diaper and put the babe in a sling contraption tied around her neck then went out to milk Belle.

Thirty minutes later, she patiently spooned milk into Allie's mouth. She returned the babe to the sling and trudged out to hitch the plow to her mule. Time to plant a garden if they expected to eat.

Halfway through the plowing, she stopped and leaned against the mule to catch her breath. A spindly tree no more than five feet high that stood at the edge of the homestead snagged her attention. It might be the only tree as far as the eye could see, but the branches spread wide as though challenging the wind to rip it out by the roots. She'd often wondered who'd planted it. Other nesters? Had they been dreamers who yearned for a bit of shade?

She'd noticed the tree before but had never heard it whisper in the wind. Never heard it call her name. Until now.

Speak your heart it seemed to say.

As though in a trance, she dropped the mule's reins and went into the soddy. Finding a scrap of paper, she dipped a goose quill into a small bottle of ink.

> *Dear God, I fear I'm going mad like Mrs. Fletcher. This blessed silence is a curse. Dead dreams and solitude fill the unending days. I yearn for a touch, a smile, and the sound of another human voice. I long to be loved, cherished, kissed. To know I matter.*

After punching a hole in the paper, she found a piece of yarn. Marching across the partially plowed furrows, she tied the paper onto a tree limb.

No one would ever read her scribbles. No one would ever hear her heart's hope, but she felt a calm wash over her for having voiced her thoughts. Feeling somewhat renewed, she tried to spoon more milk into Allie's rosebud mouth before returning to her plow.

* * *

During the night, a snarling pack of coyotes awakened Maura. They were very close to the soddy. She rose and lit the lamp. Snatching up a loaded Winchester that had belonged to her husband, she opened the door about six inches. At least half a dozen pairs or more of glittering yellow eyes stared back at her. The way they bared their razor sharp teeth and lunged at each other's throats they had to be from rival packs.

She stilled her trembles. Opening the door a little wider, she aimed at the predators and pulled the trigger. One went down. Three of the pack pounced on their brother, snarling. Orange flame shot from the barrel of her rifle again, then again. At last, pulling the dead coyote, they retreated into the safety of darkness.

Fear crawled up her spine. They were still out there whether she could see them or not. And they sensed her terror. They'd kill her without hesitation.

Holding the lantern up high, she inched toward a large dark form lying several yards away. Her cow? Relief made her knees weak when she found it was a dead antelope the coyote pack had brought down.

A quick glance at the barn assured her she'd remembered to bar the door earlier to keep Belle safe for the night. She couldn't take any chances with Allie's only milk supply.

Allie! She had to get back to Baby Girl.

But she had herself to think about also. This meat would feed her for weeks. Her clothes hung on her because she'd had so little to eat.

Did she dare to fight the vicious coyotes for what she could salvage?

Without hesitation, she grabbed the antelope's hind leg and yanked. Halfway to the soddy, the coyotes started closing in. They would risk death to get the fresh carcass.

She put the rifle to her shoulder and fired. One lunged at her and she shot it. Bone-chilling snarls echoed in the night air.

Unable to remember how many shots she'd fired, panic gripped her. If she ran out, they'd swoop in for the kill.

Maybe she should abandon the antelope and let them have it.

Yet, Allie's life and hers depended on this food. She'd not quit. She couldn't.

She tightened her grip and using her remaining strength managed to drag the antelope up next to the wall of the soddy.

No time to rest her aching muscles. She hurried inside for a sharp knife and began cutting off chunks of the meat while keeping one eye out for the desperate, hungry predators.

By the time rosy ribbons of light finally spread over the land, she'd washed off the blood and went in to feed Allie. The babe had become even more listless and that struck fear so deep into Maura's soul she couldn't breathe. Over the course of an hour, she managed to trickle some nourishment at least into the child's open mouth without strangling her. But she needed more.

Sobbing with frustration, Maura had to find a better way of getting milk into Baby Girl or else dig a grave. Ice swept up her spine.

Maura gathered her sharp knife and again tempted fate, going out to harvest the antelope's stomach. She'd heard tales of such things serving as a feeding implement for babies. Willing to try anything, she gently removed the stomach and formed a makeshift pouch by sewing it tight with some of the animal's sinew. Several washings with hot water made it ready for use. She quickly filled it with milk.

Minutes later, Allie sucked greedily from a pinhole left unbound. Once full, the babe gave her a weak smile. This was going to work. Maura said a quick prayer of thanks and knew just how to share her joy.

* * *

That morning Maura got out her paper and wrote:

Thanks be to God from whom all blessings flow. I have food and I've pushed death from my door yet again. I won't let it have my baby. I won't let it silence my hope. I vow to fight to the last breath.

Trudging across the furrowed garden to the little tree, she tied it to a branch. Now two notes fluttered in the breeze like little doves carrying messages. She desperately wanted one to return with a green leaf, an olive branch, some hope of better times like the bird once had to Noah.

Maura stared across the unending waves of brown grass that stretched as far as the eye could see.

She needed to believe. She needed a relief from toil and exhaustion.

Most of all she needed to feel alive again. To dream.

This couldn't be all there was. There had to be more.

* * *

Though exhausted by the long previous night, she kept busy. When dusk came she thought back over her day and all she'd accomplished. The dead carcasses lay well out of range of the soddy for the wild animals to finish devouring. Her food stores were replenished.

The antelope stew with its thick juice simmering on the stove filled the dwelling with a delicious aroma. She moved over to stir it, remembering the joy she took from serving this dish to her dear husband. Of course, they'd had cornbread to go with it then. She'd had plenty of flour and meal in those days.

He'd come in after a full day's work, sniff the air and a big smile would spread across his face easing the tired lines. Then he'd put his arms around her and nuzzle her neck. Tell her how much he loved her.

Oh God, how she missed that man.

She brushed away a tear and glanced over at Allie. Maura had fed her every two hours. Color had begun to come back into the babe's wan little face, a testament the makeshift bottle would do its job.

Before complete darkness descended, Maura got out her paper and tore off another piece.

Is there anyone out there? Am I and my baby the only ones left on this earth? I desperately need to know for my own sanity, to hope.

When she closed her eyes in sleep, she dreamed of a man with laughing gray eyes and strong callused hands.

* * *

The image stayed with her when she awakened. Who was this man of her dreams? Her husband's eyes had been dark brown and he'd had a withered hand.

A strange sound met her ears.

A baby's coos.

Maura peered into the wooden cradle. Allie was staring at her hand and cooing.

"Hey there, little darlin'. How's my girl? I hope you're hungry because I'll have some warm milk as soon as I get Belle in the mood of giving." Tears stung her eyes. She laid back on the pillow, contemplating this wonderful gift she'd been given.

And so began her day. After feeding Allie, she put the child in the sling around her chest and went to work. She had to get seed into the ground. More spring rain would hopefully come and she wanted to have her plot of land ready.

But before she got started, she tied her late-night note onto the little scraggly tree. In a way, it was like talking to God. No one would ever read them, but they helped relieve her frustration and voice the deep loneliness that seeped into her soul.

With the notes rustling in the wind murmuring words of hope, she went about the job of living.

* * *

The next morning after feeding Allie and herself, she got out her writing implements.

I dreamed of strong arms around me, holding me with love. Am I destined to never know that again? I yearn to hear another's heart beating softly next to me, feel his touch on my body. I cannot bear the thought of living the rest of my days all alone.

Once more, she tied it to the tree. Then she jerked back.

One note did not belong to her. It had a bright red string. She always used a length of gray yarn.

Who could've put this strange one there?

Maura quickly glanced around, scanning the flat land. Nothing. No evidence of another human within sight.

Nothing but this note to say another had walked near.

Her trembling fingers fumbled with the red string. At last she got it untied it and read:

You are not alone. I am here. I care. You matter to someone. You matter to me.

A tear trickled silently down her cheek. Someone felt her pain and took the time to let her know. She carefully retied it to the branch and again surveyed the area. Still no movement anywhere.

Over the next three weeks, Maura and this mysterious person conversed back and forth. She learned his name was Sam and that he worked for Western Union Telegraph Company as a lineman in charge of repairing broken telegraph poles and downed lines. She savored each of the lonely widower's messages.

One of Sam's notes read:

> *If wishes were dreams I would hold you in my arms, darling Maura, and never let you go. Each time the sun goes down I kiss you goodnight and dream of your beautiful face. What do you wish for, pretty lady?*

She quickly penned a reply.

> *Sam, you don't know how much you've come to mean to me. My wish would be for your strong arms around me, your lips on mine, our hearts beating as one. I dream of meeting you beneath the stars and walking hand in hand across the heavens.*

Their conversations through the notes brought Maura much comfort and strength. Though they never met, she developed a deep abiding love for this man.

Each morning she couldn't wait to visit the tree and see the new notes waving gaily in the breeze. He was the green leaf, the olive branch she'd desperately wanted to find.

Her heart skipped several beats when she received this one:

What is the face of love to you, dearest Maura?

To which she immediately replied:

It's what's inside a person's heart, deep down past the scars of hurt and grief. You wear the face of love, darling Sam.

Maura floated through the days, feeling loved and cherished. Sam was the answer to her heart's yearning. He'd given her strength and hope and courage. No task was too difficult or impossible. His words of love made her feel like a woman again. She'd almost forgotten what that felt like.

Then one day this message came that shocked her to her core:

> *My job in this part of Texas is over. They're sending me to Julesburg, Colorado Territory. I'm sorry. Knowing you has eased my deep loneliness. I wish you well, dearest Maura. Think of me from time to time with fondness as I will you. When the wind blows from the west and gently brushes your face it'll be my fingers caressing you.*

Pain doubled her over. He was gone. Maura fell into the cushion of tall grass weeping. Once again, she had no one to talk to, to share the lonely day's struggles with.

No one to care.

Sam had surely died also even though she had no grave to visit.

* * *

One month went by then two more with each day crawling straight into the next.

Nothing to break the monotony.

Nothing to ease the isolation.

Nothing to bring solace when the rigors of life beat her down.

After carefully removing each note, Maura tucked them safely away and avoided the place that had brought her much happiness.

Yet, when the morning sun's golden rays caressed the outstretched branches of the sad little tree, she paused for just a moment remembering the man named Sam who had taught her to dream again. She'd felt his touch, his kisses even though they'd existed solely in words.

Because of Sam and the strength he'd given her, she was able to go about the business of living and caring for her darling daughter. He'd given Maura much more than he knew. And when the wind blew from the west, she felt him watching over her.

Allie grew and continued to thrive. The child babbled continuously. Maura taught her to say "Mama" and made a point to laugh at her silly antics.

On a sweltering summer morning in August, she casually glanced out the window while she prepared breakfast.

Something waved from the little tree. Her imagination played a cruel joke on her for sure. Still, Maura ran outside to get a better look.

Shielding her eyes against the sun, she could barely see a glimpse of red, but it was there. Trembling, she grabbed Allie and raced across the small field from which rows of corn, squash, turnips and other vegetables grew.

When she drew closer, she saw a man sitting beneath the branches, propped up against the trunk. He grinned wide.

She slowed to a walk. What if this stranger had evil on his mind? Her rifle still rested on the wall of the soddy.

Something inside told her to keep going.

His laughing gray eyes held kindness like the man in her dream. A voice whispered she had nothing to fear. Five yards away from him, he pushed to his feet. He stood over six feet tall.

"Sam? Sam, is it you?"

"It's me. I've wanted to meet you for a long time, Maura." He held out his hand. "Come here."

In a daze, Maura lowered Allie to the grass then went into his welcoming arms. "I thought I lost you," she whispered.

"I found that no matter how hard I tried, you're impossible to forget. I had to get back here. I quit my job and rode night and day to get here. I was afraid my ugly face would frighten you. That's why I didn't come to the house and knock on the door either today—or all those times when we tied our messages to the Telegraph Tree here."

The Telegraph Tree. What an apt name.

She stepped one foot back to drink in the sight of him. A long scar ran from his cheek to his square jaw, but she'd never felt safer. She took his hands and ran her fingers across the big calluses. "You are a handsome man and don't frighten me one bit. My heart already knows you."

He brushed his lips across her cheek. "Your eyes are the color of freshly-turned earth. You are my angel, beautiful Maura."

Her pulse sang through her veins.

"Sam, this may sound odd, but I dreamt of you before we ever started corresponding. At the time, though, it made no sense to me."

"It must've been Heaven's way of an introduction. The Good Lord appears to be an architect in these matters." Sam knelt to say hello to Allie and brush her soft golden curls. "I used to hide in the tall grass and watch you both. I saw how hard you worked and wished for the courage to knock on your door. You're the kind of woman I always wanted, nothing like the others who could barely stomach the sight of me after I came back from war."

Maura's heart broke for him. "Let's forget the past. We've had too much sorrow."

Sam rose and gently caressed Maura's cheek. "Do you mind if I kiss you?"

"I thought you'd never ask," she whispered.

Tenderly, he put his large hands on both sides of her face and pressed his lips to hers. At that instant, Maura knew she didn't want to be anywhere but in his arms.

It was like a beautiful dream. If that's all it was, she didn't want to wake up.

She got out the notes she'd kept. With his help, she tied them all back on along with new ones each of them penned. The tree was awash with glorious color and hopeful dreams.

They discussed marriage and the fact it would take a long time to be wed. Neither wanted to wait six months or a year.

An old symbolic custom came to mind for just such a situation. Maura turned to him. "Let's jump the broom, Sam."

That evening as the sun floated low on the horizon, Maura and Sam pledged their love for all eternity beneath the limbs of their tree. Then laying the broom on the ground, they held hands and, taking a big leap, jumped over it.

Allie Rose, who refused to budge from Sam's arms, laughed and clapped as though she understood everything.

And maybe she did.

MOON DOG NIGHT

~Part One~

The frigid night air settled around Bonner Raine's shoulders, promising a miserable night. He tugged the collar of his coat up against his neck and moved closer to the fire. Shivering, he glanced up at the winter sky and the large halo around the moon. Over to the left of the bright orb was a moon dog just as sure as he was freezing his rear off.

"Snow's coming. Bet it'll be here before morning," he told his hound.

Jezzie yawned and curled up next to Bonner. She was part cow dog and part wolf. A mixture just like him. They suited each other—pieces of different things put together to make a whole.

Bonner leaned back against his saddle and drew his hat down low over his eyes. He prayed he could get a little sleep before he had to ride. He was Lord almighty weary of this life of hunting bad men. Folks shot him looks of disdain when he rode into towns, leading a horse with some desperate outlaw slung belly-down over it. They said Bonner was no more than a killer—all because he collected rewards for ridding the world of evil.

Not all of the wanted men chose to die. He always gave them a choice. Never once in the time he'd been at this had he shot anyone without offering them a choice—jail or the grave—then let the cards play out how they were dealt.

For the most part, men on the run were short in the brain department. The majority tried to outshoot him rather than go to jail peaceable. But one day, Bonner's luck would end. He knew that as sure as he was sitting there.

The fire crackled and popped and somewhere off in the distance a lonely coyote howled. He pulled his bedroll over him.

Way he saw it, he was no different from a lawman who administered justice for free. They both accomplished the same thing and getting paid for it provided Bonner with a living.

But he was tired of dodging bullets and outrunning the devil. Not much of a life for a man with dreams. He had his eye on a little farm in the Texas Hill Country where one day he could settle down with a good woman and raise a crop of kids. That is if he could find someone who could put up with the demons that shared Bonner's saddle.

One more outlaw and he'd have enough money.

The capture of Billy Osage could buy that farm.

Thoughts of that piece of land meandered through his mind as he let his hand drift over Jezzie's black and white fur. She never judged and was loyal to a fault. Just then he caught the whinny of a horse beyond the firelight and raised, listening. Jezzie growled and stood. Bonner flung the bedroll aside and lurched to his feet, drawing his Colt. Keeping low, he crept to the edge of darkness and took cover in the brush. Jezzie raced into the black night, raising holy hell.

Quiet voices reached him as though nothing more than a sigh of the cold wind. But Bonner trusted his instincts. Someone was out there.

He waited and watched. Over the last six years he'd seen every trick known and some that weren't. Jezzie had become oddly silent. What had happened to the hound?

A horse shuffled its feet. More whispers.

"Show yourself," Bonner growled.

At last, came a child's voice. "Don't shoot, mister."

"Come on in," Bonner called. "Slow and easy."

He stayed hidden in case Osage had stooped to using a kid to lure him into the open. Nothing that outlaw did would surprise Bonner. Not one damn thing.

A rustle of brush preceded the visitor. When the mule stepped into the circle of light with Jezzie plodding alongside, he stared in shock.

The riders were kids—two of them—the oldest no more than nine or ten.

* * *

His Colt in hand, Bonner rose and scanned the darkness. He waited for Billy Osage to race toward him with gun blazing—or at the very least the parents of these children.

"Tell anybody with you to come out, kid." Now in the light, he noticed the oldest was a boy. Behind him, gripping the boy's waist, was a little girl with long blonde hair. She gave a loud sniffle.

"Ain't nobody with us," said the boy. "Just me and my sister. We're cold. Hungry."

Bonner slid his Colt into the holster. "What are you doing out here all by yourself?" He helped the kids to the ground and moved them by the fire. The boy could barely walk for the heavy pistol stuck in the waist of his pants. Thank goodness both wore thick coats.

The boy shot him a wary glance and held his hands to the flame. "Lookin' for somebody, mister."

"Call me Bonner. Bonner Raine. Are you lost?"

"Nope."

"Got a name, kid?" Bonner was trying to make sense of this. If he was dreaming, he wished he'd wake up. Surely they were a figment of his imagination. He'd been dog tired down to his bones before, but never where he saw ghosts.

"Jonathan Timothy Andrew Cutler."

"I'm Addie," said the girl shyly. Jezzie whimpered and licked her hand.

"Well, Jonathan Timothy Andrew Cutler and Addie, if I knew who you were looking for I could help you find them." Bonner glanced at the mule and found bedrolls tied to the animal and a burlap sack filled with something hanging from the saddle horn. The kids had prepared for a trip, not just a spur of the moment ride.

"Aimin' to find Billy Osage. He killed our papa. Took our mama." Jonathan glanced up. The blue flames of the fire shone on his grim young features. Anger glistened in his dark eyes and hardened his voice. "I'm gonna get her back. An' I'm gonna kill Billy Osage."

As soon as Bonner got over the shock of the statement, he whistled through his teeth. "That's a mighty tall order, Jonathan." He didn't doubt the commitment though. This kid sure as shooting had his mind set on going up against the most ruthless outlaw in Texas—and he wouldn't stand a chance.

"We gonna git our mama," little Addie said. Bonner guessed her age to be about five. She reached for her brother's hand and clenched it. Tiptoeing to reach his ear, she whispered loudly, "I'm hungry, Jonathan."

Bonner kicked himself for not asking if they'd eaten. He glanced at the still warm skillet that held a rabbit stew he'd thrown together. "You're welcome to my stew. I made plenty."

"We ain't askin' for charity," Jonathan said firmly. But Bonner saw the boy cast a sideways glance at the pan. Addie was downright staring.

"Listen, you'd be doing me a favor. Me and my dog have eaten all we can hold and I'll have to throw it out." When he saw hesitation in their eyes, he grabbed a tin plate and filled it then got two spoons. "You'll have to share the plate. Sorry."

They sat on his bedroll and the way they dug in said they were starving. Jezzie laid down beside Addie. It seemed the girls were going to stick together in this.

"When did Billy Osage come by your place?" Bonner asked, pouring himself a cup of coffee.

"This morning," Jonathan muttered around his chewing. "About sunrise. Me an' Addie hid in the hayloft."

29

"How do you know it was Osage?"

"On account of what he said right before he shot our papa between the eyes. 'Tell the devil Billy Osage sent you.' He jerked Mama onto a horse and they lit out with her screaming."

Bonner narrowed his eyes over the rim of the cup. That sounded like the low-down, no-account outlaw. "Did you ever see him before today?"

"Nope." The boy wiped his mouth on a bandana that he took from around his neck then wiped Addie's face.

Jezzie's eyes found Bonner's and she whimpered as though pleading for him to help these children. The dog didn't need to ask. He'd already decided and not because he needed Billy Osage's carcass for the reward. He'd do it to give the children back their mother and right the wrong.

"That man is a mighty mean hombre. Think you can get justice and rescue your mama by yourself?"

"Yep." Jonathan set down the plate they'd cleaned and went to the mule.

Bonner followed. "Need some help?"

"Nope." The kid dragged a rock over to stand on and untied two bedrolls—and a yarn-headed doll. Stalking back, he thrust the doll at Addie, then spread out their bedrolls. Bonner watched in amazement. The boy was sure self-sufficient and determined not to ask for help.

While he admired that, he wanted to shake the boy. He and his sister had no business being out here chasing Billy Osage in the dead of winter. With a snowstorm likely bearing down.

The kid might shoot his fool self with that pistol weighing down his pants. "How did you track the outlaw anyway, son?"

"My papa was a Texas Ranger and he taught me. Taught me a lot of stuff."

"How to shoot?" Bonner asked.

"Yep."

"There's a lot of difference in aiming at things that can't shoot back. Have you ever killed a man, Jonathan?"

"Nope. But I will." Jonathan took little Addie to the bushes. When he stalked back, he laid down next to his sister and covered them.

Bonner reckoned the boy had chewed all the fat he was going to for now. He'd wait until the kid went to sleep, then he'd take that gun before it accidentally went off.

But, just as he finished the thought, Jonathan pulled the pistol out and hid it somewhere deep in the folds of the bedroll. Bonner silently cussed a blue streak. It was almost as if the pint-sized lawman had read his mind.

Bonner sat there thinking a long time after he heard the boy's snores. Anger rose so thick it almost choked him. He and Osage were going to have a long conversation—as soon as he got these kids' mother from the outlaw's clutches.

Jezzie rose from a spot beside Addie and laid down next to Bonner. The dog glanced up and whimpered.

"I know, girl. We've got to fix this." Bonner tossed another piece of wood onto the fire and watched it spark and sizzle. He was deep into plans when the unmistakable sound of sobs reached him. He got to his feet to see what he could do to comfort, although he was pretty rusty in that department.

Addie lay next to her sleeping brother, crying her heart out. Bonner lifted her into his arms and patted her back. "There, tell me what's wrong, sweet girl."

"I want my mama. She always gives me a goodnight kiss."

"Honey, I'm sorry she's not here to do that, but I promise that we're going to find her." Worry niggled in Bonner's head as a thought froze him. Unless Osage killed her. What then? It would be typical for the outlaw. What would he do with these kids?

He sat down and held her in his lap until she fell asleep sucking her thumb. Tenderness rose from a place so far down inside Bonner he hadn't known it existed. His eyes narrowed.

Billy Osage was a dead man.

With a long sigh, he tucked Addie back into the bedroll and put her doll in her arms, covering the children with a warm blanket.

Bonner dropped back onto his bedroll. A glance at the sky revealed the clouds that had formed overhead, blocking the moon. Flakes of snow touched his face.

* * *

Snow covered everything when Bonner woke just a little before daybreak. Light from the fire showed

33

only the sleeping little girl. He jerked to his feet. That little rascal. Where was Jonathan? Jezzie rose from her place next to Addie and stretched. The fool dog was supposed to alert him. Hell!

Bonner moved to the horses, praying the mule would still be there. He caught Jonathan mounting up. "Going somewhere?" Bonner asked quietly.

The kid turned. "To find Mama."

"And leave your little sister behind? I thought your father would've taught you better." Bonner heard doubt creek into Jonathan's voice for the first time and knew the kid wrestled with that.

"Figure she's safe enough. She ain't got any business where there's killing."

"You mean when you put a bullet into Billy Osage?"

"Yep."

"Can't let you leave by yourself, son. Climb down and eat something." Bonner offered a hand. "Family sticks together—through good and bad."

With a curt nod, Jonathan walked back to the campfire. While Bonner fixed a bite of breakfast, the boy got Addie up and took her to the bushes. They ate the quick meal in silence. Bonner's thoughts were on killing Billy Osage, figured the boy's were too.

In quick order, Bonner broke down the camp. Little Addie rode in front of Bonner where he held her secure and in front of her was Jezzie. They were moving too fast for the dog to keep up.

Drifts of heavy snow covered the trail but Bonner needed no sign to lead him to Osage's hideout. Outlaws were creatures of habit. They went to places they knew best and felt safe—only the man would find no place in Texas safe from him.

This would be a day of reckoning and the price would be steep.

Each step their mounts took, Bonner prayed they'd find Mrs. Cutler alive. He couldn't bear to consider the alternative or what would happen to these children. He cast Jonathan a glance and found the boy staring straight ahead, his jaw clenched. The kid was going to make a heck of a lawman—if he lived long enough.

Bonner considered it his job to make certain he did.

They dismounted about five hundred yards from Osage's shack. They'd leave the animals and he and the boy would go on foot. He crouched down and brushed the hair from Addie's eyes. "Honey, listen good. You have to stay with Jezzie. She'll take care of you. Whatever happens, don't move from here. You understand? All our lives depend on that."

"But I wanna come."

Jonathan knelt to wipe her nose. "Dang it, Addie. I told you it's too dangerous. You'll get mama killed. You cry too much and—" he glanced around. Finally, picking up her doll he thrust it into his sister's hands. "Take care of Bessie. She needs you. Do not follow me."

The boy glanced at Bonner as though seeming to say that he'd do this alone. Tough. He was going whether the kid wanted him there or not.

Their breath fogged in the air as he and Jonathan crept through the snow-covered brush with guns in hand. Bonner stared at the shack where a thin column of smoke rose from the chimney. He had to see inside. "I'm going to take a look. You stay here and don't fire that pistol. You do and your mother is dead."

If she wasn't already but Bonner kept that to himself.

"No, I'm smaller and can hug the ground," Jonathan insisted.

The kid had a point. Bonner pinched the bridge of his nose and cussed a silent blue streak. "All right. I'll provide cover in case you need it. Don't go off half-cocked on me. Just look and get right back so we can figure out a plan."

Jonathan glared. "If Billy has a gun on my mama, I'm shooting."

Before Bonner could reason with him, the boy sprinted to a tree. Running from one trunk to the next, Jonathan reached a window of the hideout and peered inside. Bonner would give a year's reward money to know what the boy saw. Keeping low, the kid moved to a second window and raised for a look. Evidently, satisfied, he ran back to Bonner.

"Mama's tied up on a bed an' Billy Osage's eatin' at a table," Jonathan said. "I'll bet he didn't feed her nothing."

"Draw out the room in the snow and where she is located." Bonner prayed she'd be strong enough to walk under her own power. Once the shooting started, he might not have time to do more than untie her.

He studied the layout Jonathan drew in the snow. "Okay, here's the plan. When you're in place at a window, I'll burst through the front door at a run and catch Osage by surprise. Don't fire toward your mother. And don't shoot me."

Lord, this was a dumb plan. Maybe the outlaw would be so confused he wouldn't have time to go for his gun. Bonner only had the kid's word that he knew how to shoot. A wild bullet could kill him and Mrs. Cutler both. But he didn't have it in him to tie up the kid. Jonathan Timothy Andrew Cutler burned with a need for justice. He deserved a chance to get it. Bonner would feel the same if he walked in Jonathan's shoes.

Once the boy was back at the window and Bonner had positioned himself closer, he took a deep breath. Gripping his Navy Colt, he ran for the door and burst through the rotted wood. A woman's scream rent the air. Billy Osage jumped to his feet, drawing. Bonner fired, striking the outlaw's shoulder, spinning him around. Another bullet broke through the window and hit the outlaw square between the eyes. Osage fell like rock. Bonner slid his smoking gun into the holster and went to the children's mother.

"Bless you, mister. He meant to kill me. I've got to get home to my children." Her voice was shaky.

Bonner wiped blood from her face, noticing the bruises. "The kids are here, ma'am. Your son fired the shot that killed Billy Osage."

Just then Jonathan ran inside and hugged his mother. Bonner turned to go get Addie, but the little girl met him at the door. So much for staying put.

"Mama! Mama!" she screamed, rushing past him.

Jonathan moved to Bonner, his solemn dark eyes revealing the pain of shooting his first man. The boy stuck out his hand.

Bonner shook it. "Your father would be proud of you, kid. Everything he taught you paid off and you got your mama back just like you said you would. I'm proud of you too. Not many men could've tracked Osage and then shot him dead between the eyes."

"Thanks, Mr. Raine."

"I'll help you get the body into town but the reward money belongs to you. It'll help ease your burden for a bit."

So much for staying put. Jezzie nuzzled his hand. The dog hadn't minded either. Bonner shook his head then turned to watch the happy reunion. Everything had turned out.

His farm slipped from reach—for now. There were plenty more outlaws to bring in. They were like roaches—stomp one and another rose to take his place.

One day, if the cards played out right, he'd have his dream. Just a matter of time.

~Part Two~

Over the next year, Bonner and Jezzie would swing by to check on Mrs. Cutler and the two kids whenever he found himself in the vicinity. Each time, Rebecca would invite him to sit down to supper and offer some sweet-smelling hay in the barn to bed down on.

His mind took to wandering there even when he was nowhere close.

With good reason. Rebecca Cutler was a fine-looking woman with kind ways. She was too young to keep a farm going and raise two children alone.

The cinnamon sky had begun to darken when he rode up to the farmhouse. Jezzie danced around his paint's hooves, excited to see her young friend.

Rebecca hurried out, wiping her hands on her apron, a smile lighting up her face. "I declare, Bonner, I think you smelled my fried chicken."

"Yes, ma'am." He eased his weary bones from the saddle. "That would purely be hard to miss. I'll wash up."

"Mr. Bonner! Jezzie!" Addie ran around her mother. "Oh boy!"

The little girl launched herself into his arms. He nuzzled her neck and hugged her tight, breathing in her innocence. He didn't want to stain her with the blood on his hands and the things he was forced to do to stay alive but he couldn't keep from holding her close. He wasn't that strong.

"I missed you, girl."

"I have a kitty. Wanna see?"

"I sure do. When I get washed up, you can show me." He set her down and she hugged Jezzie, burying her face in the soft fur.

"Addie, I need your help. Let Bonner get the trail dust washed off," her mother called. Addie scampered to the porch with Jezzie at her side.

He moved toward the barn with his big paint. "Guess you'll be wanting your oats, Chief." The brown and white paint snorted and tossed his head.

"I'll take him, Bonner," Jonathan said, taking the reins. "I'm glad you came."

"Boy, I think you've grown a foot! Pretty soon, you'll be as tall as me." Bonner's gaze swept over the eleven-year-old. The sadness in his dark eyes made him appear a boy in an old man's body. It made Bonner's heart ache to watch how quickly he'd had to grow up. For a minute, he wished he could dig up the outlaw Billy Osage and shoot him again. "How've things been around here? Any problems?"

"Naw. Just work." Jonathan released a heavy sigh. "The roof's leaking and I need some help with the fence in the north pasture if you're going to stay a few days."

"Yeah. I'll stay." Even if he had someplace to be, he wouldn't. The kid didn't ask for help often. That meant they were things he couldn't handle by himself.

"I hear Mama crying sometimes. She's real sad."

For a minute, Bonner thought he'd imagined the boy's low words.

"I wonder if you could talk to her," Jonathan added, clarifying things in Bonner's mind.

"Sure. I'll do my best to see what's wrong, but it might be nothing more than missing your papa." He draped an arm across the boy's thin shoulders. "You worry too much about grown up things. When was the last time you ever had any fun?"

"Too much to do. I gotta be the man now." Jonathan walked on to the barn with Chief.

Bonner's gaze followed him for a long moment before he pumped some water from the well and set about the business of making himself presentable at Rebecca's table. He might be a tad short of flowery language but he did possess manners.

A fine woman like her needed to be respected.

After that ... how in the hell would he go about talking to her of delicate things?

* * *

No question about it, the meal was delicious and the company made all his lonely nights by a campfire seem like purgatory.

Addie got from her seat and took his hand. "Come see my kitty, Mr. Bonner."

She led him to a box in the barn and lifted up a flea-bitten calico that had been nursing on its mama. "Ain't she purty?"

"Why she sure is." He held the kitten against him. "What did you name her?"

Jonathan stole up behind them. "She tried to name the fur ball Orin after Daddy. Then I explained it was a girl cat and she settled on Alice."

"I did not." Addie pouted and put her hands on her hips.

"Did too."

"That's enough," Bonner said quietly. "It doesn't make a hill of beans." He handed Addie the kitten. "Put her back with her mama and let's get you to bed."

When Rebecca came from tucking Addie in, Bonner rose from his chair. "It's a nice night. Let's stroll over to the corral where we can look at the stars."

"That's sounds real fine, Bonner." She lifted her coat from a nail and Bonner held it for her.

Moments later, his boots crunched on the rocky ground of the Texas Hill Country. He placed a hand on the small of her back as they strolled toward the windmill that rose tall in the darkness. Although she was a small woman, she had a spine of pure steel. Women could allow little softness in this wild land or they'd never survive. From what he'd heard, Bonner suspected she was close to reaching her limit. Maybe it was time to speak of things he'd held back.

"I always love the sound of this old windmill." Rebecca leaned her head on his shoulder and the vanilla she'd used in making the fresh apple cake she'd served for dessert drifted to his nose.

"Windmills always take me home." Bonner frowned. *Fool.* Couldn't he think of something better to say? "Growing up, I had one right out my upstairs loft. It sang me to sleep many a night." He glanced up at it and noticed one of the blades needed tightened. One more chore to add to his list.

She stared out into the night as though she'd be unable to get the words out if she glanced up at

45

him. "You look real tired, Bonner. Each time you ride out, I worry you won't come back, that a bullet will find you." Her voice caught in a strangled sob. "Quit this dangerous job while you still can."

He faced her and took her shoulders. "Rebecca, what's wrong?"

"Everything. Nothing. I should've known Jonathan would hear and tell you." She glanced up with tears in her eyes. "I don't know how long I can hold on to this patch of ground. I'm so lonely and sometimes every part of my being yearns for a gentle touch, to hear another breathing next to me. To share the load."

"I figured as much. It's got to be hard."

"This land, the emptiness is draining the life from me and Jonathan is more like sixty than a twelve-year-old. It breaks my heart. I see no choice but move into town. I could get a job as a laundress or maid. For Jonathan and Addie."

He touched her cheek with his fingertips, cursing the roughness. "Marry me, Rebecca. Let me take your burdens. We can be a family and the children can have a father. I'll quit hunting vermin." He paused for a long moment. "A man like me doesn't know flowery words. I'm plainspoken but I love you and I want you to be my wife."

Surprise shot across her face. "You love me? Are you sure?"

He lifted a silky tendril of hair and rubbed it between his fingers. "I've long wanted to tell you but I don't have anything to offer. Nothing but myself. If that's enough—"

"Oh, Bonner, you're more than enough. I'll be proud to walk by your side." She cupped his jaw with a touch so tender it made his breath hitch. "I love you, you know. I have for a long time."

This was news to him but he knew she'd never say those words if she didn't mean them.

He drew her against him, lowered his head, and placed his lips on hers. The kiss spoke of promises and all the sweet tomorrows that would come. They'd raise the kids and grow old together. They'd make each day count for something. And they'd never suffer in lonely silence again.

The lines from a song drifted through his head. *Anyone can make you happy by doing something special. But only someone special can make you happy by doing nothing.*

And Rebecca was his sun and moon and stars all rolled into one.

THE GUNSLINGER

~Chapter 1~

Southwest Texas 1881

Her father had always warned her of how hot hell would be if she didn't walk the straight and narrow. Him being a man of the cloth, and on a personal level with such things, she figured he'd known a lot about that particular subject seeing as how he steered from the path at every turn.

And she fervently agreed about the inhospitable temperature.

If ever there was a hell, this would be it.

Skye O'Rourke brushed back hair that stuck to the sweat on her face and took in the shimmering horizon. The desert landscape baked under the sun like a piece of old buffalo hide.

God, how she hated this land and the incessant wind that dried crops and people, turning them to nothing but dust.

Weary and heartsore, Skye rested her forehead on the fencepost that she struggled to set back into the ground. At that moment, she hated Matthew O'Rourke for dying, for leaving her all alone, for bringing her to this desolate place.

And she cursed the blessed hopelessness that had squeezed out softness and dreams and laughter.

But most of all, it was the endless quiet that filled her days. The only thing to break the silence was the creak of the windmill that sang its own sad song, the pitiful lowing of her sick milk cow, and the occasional cluck of a chicken running loose in her yard.

Sometimes, she feared she was losing her mind.

The yearning to hear another voice rose up so strong at times it almost strangled her.

This was no kind of life for a woman. If only she had somewhere to go and money to get there, she'd pack up and head back East. Some place far from the Texas desert. Some place where life was easier. Someplace that didn't age a woman so quickly.

Sweat trickled down between her breasts soaking her bodice. Skye undid the buttons until she reached the frayed ribbon on her chemise underneath. It didn't matter. Nothing much mattered. No one would see her even if she were to strip off her dress.

Impatiently, she shoved the fabric aside, desperate for a bit of cooling breeze against her parched skin.

Thickness clogged her throat. How could she go on? And who would care if she couldn't?

Movement in the distance caught her attention. She shaded her eyes from the sun. The tall figure of a man with a gun belt hanging low around his hips walked slowly toward her. He had something slung over his shoulder.

A saddle?

Why would a man walk in this heat?

Had she finally gone stark-raving mad, seeing a vision only in her mind? She closed her eyes then looked again. Only he was still there and getting closer.

Was this some new ploy of her enemy, Hiram Dunston?

The man terrified her. He'd started coming around after her husband died, trying to force himself on her. She'd been forced to shoot him, wounding him in the shoulder. Now, Hiram was hell-bent on destroying her. Two nights, he'd ripped out every fencepost along the front of her property. She also felt certain he'd sickened her milk cow and set fire to a wagon around back. Thank goodness, the wagon hadn't been in the barn. She shuddered to think how she'd manage if she lost her horse.

Erring on the side of caution, she strode to the house and reached inside for Matthew's old rifle she kept next to the door. It didn't shoot very straight, but at least it might scare off the man. She set her jaw. If it did turn out to be Hiram, she'd aim for his privates this time.

Skye raised the rifle to her shoulder and was about to order the stranger to stop when he staggered and went down to his knees in the dirt.

For several long beats of her heart, he struggled to rise. At last, he made it to his feet and once more shouldered the weight of the saddle. She dropped the rifle and ran to help, no longer afraid that he posed a threat.

"Water," he croaked when she reached his side.

Up close, his face resembled a piece of cooked leather. He stared at her with eyes that had glazed over from the heat.

"Let's get you to the house, mister. Leave your saddle. We'll come back for it."

"No. All I have."

"Fine." She draped his free arm around her shoulders. "Lean on me."

When they stumbled into the shadow of the sod house, he collapsed. His hat fell off, revealing hair the color of midnight. She tugged the saddle from his grasp and hurried to the well. Pumping water into a pail, she ran back and handed him a cup full.

"Sip slowly. Too much will choke you."

The stranger paid no heed, gulping it down. He dipped the cup in the pail next to him and refilled it. Once more, he downed it in several big swallows. Then he dumped what remained in the bucket over his head. It ran down, drenching his hair and black shirt.

At last, he glanced up and croaked, "Skye?"

"Who are you, mister, and how do you know my name?"

"You don't recognize me," he rasped. "I'm not surprised. It's been a few years." He took a shaky breath. "Although, there was once a time I didn't think you'd ever forget me."

He looked vaguely familiar; something about those eyes the color of a deep silent pool of crystal water. The high cheekbones and set of his jaw resembled Matthew.

A jolt ran through her. She inhaled sharply. "Cade?"

A rough chuckle squeezed from his throat. "In the flesh. Where's Matthew?"

"Don't you know? He's dead." Her voice hardened. "I wrote. Asked you to come. You didn't."

Shock rippled across his face and pain darkened his eyes. He touched his stubbled jaw. "It would've been hard for a letter to find me. I ... moved around a lot. But I'm here now."

"And in a sorry state, I might add. You have no horse. The soles of your boots have holes. And I see the gun slung low on your hip. What's happened to you? Where have you been? Why did you bother to come now?" Skye hated the anger and resentment that made her spit the words out like hard pebbles in a creek bed.

Cade's anger flared as well. "I'll answer your questions in my own good time. As for why I've come ... I had nowhere else to go." He pinched the bridge of his nose. "If you want me to leave, say the word and I'll move on."

"Of course, I don't. You're Matthew's brother."

Skye gazed into those startling blue eyes that once made her dream, made her yearn, and made her want to move heaven and earth to have him lying next to her.

God help her! They still had that power.

But he'd abandoned her, told her the call of adventure was more important than her, told her to marry his brother. What kind of man did that? She'd learned a valuable lesson and she'd not give him a chance to hurt her again.

55

A sweeping glance took him in. She saw no hint of the gentleness in the man she'd once given her heart to beneath a full moon. A hardness as unyielding as the cold piece of iron in his holster had settled over him now. From his chiseled jaw and piercing gaze to the deep lines bracketing his mouth, he was someone she didn't know.

An ache spread through her. Cade had died as surely as Matthew had. They just hadn't buried him yet.

"It'll only be for a few days," he said quietly. "Then, I promise to be out of your life. Just let me rest up."

A few days could be an eternity when tempted by his nearness and her need to be held again by strong arms, to feel a heartbeat next to her in the dead of night. Skye shoved the thought aside. This thinking would destroy her. He'd made it clear he wasn't going to stick around.

"Where will you go?" Her voice was barely louder than a whisper.

Cade shrugged and worked to get to his feet. He spoke in a flat, dead voice. "One place is as good as the next, I reckon. Learned a long time ago not to get too comfortable."

"What happened?" She needed to know, to understand. "Tell me."

"I've done things." He spread his legs as though bracing himself for a blow that would knock him to his knees. "I had to become someone else. I answer to Cade Coltrain now. In certain parts of the country my name strikes fear."

"But why? Why do you want people to be afraid of you?"

"Didn't seek it. Never. Just happened. You ask a lot of questions, Skye," he said softly. "Be careful. You might not want to know the answers."

She straightened. "Are you bringing trouble to my door?"

"Not yet. I've covered my tracks."

A strangled sob rose up. It took everything she had, but she managed to swallow it back down. She'd not let him see her pain at what he'd become.

"Are you wanted?"

"Damn it, Skye. I warned you not to ask these questions."

"I simply want to know what to expect."

"Nothing. Don't expect anything from me. I'll only disappoint you."

"You're so different. What happened to the Cade I knew?"

Cade's face hardened as though carved in stone. "He died. When I sold my soul to the highest bidder."

~Chapter 2~

The shock on Skye's face bruised Cade's heart and scalded the back of this throat. Hell, why hadn't he stayed away? He wanted to take her in his arms, kiss away the sadness and despair. He hungered for her so bad it made him tremble.

God, he'd been such a fool!

"In exchange for what?" she asked.

"Some folks need certain ... abilities I have. And I'm very, very good at what I do." Cade instantly regretted his harsh tone. He wore a hard granite shell and had since he'd killed his first man. Wasn't anything he planned or wanted.

But watching the light go out in an adversary's eyes and knowing he took it eroded something deep down inside where hopes and dreams and honor lived.

And that led to others and now he couldn't stop if he wanted.

His life now called for split-second reflexes and living in the shadows one step away from death.

He doubted any of this would make sense to Skye. He had trouble reconciling it himself. Clearly, she missed the softness in the man she used to know, but Cade O'Rourke was dead and buried.

"You're looking well, Skye," he said quietly. "No kids?"

"A blessing I missed." Her gray eyes met and held his.

Cade had no trouble seeing that life had been unkind to her. Cuts, some new and some scabbed over, on her hands came from constant toil, her fingernails broken. His gaze swept her curves, pausing at the unbuttoned dress that revealed the swell of her breasts. She was still a mighty fine-looking woman. He longed to undo the braid that snaked down her back and plunge his hands in hair the color of a flaming sunset, smell her sweetness. Kiss her until all the breath left their bodies and make mad, passionate love.

"I'm sorry. I remember how you used to yearn for kids." He allowed a flicker of a smile.

"Have you eaten?" She focused on something in the distance, as though she already pictured him leaving.

"Not for a day or two. I'd be obliged."

"I'll have something ready by the time you wash up." With those curt words, she turned and disappeared into the house.

He released a heavy sigh. A sweeping glance of the homestead took in the broken fences, little livestock and no crops. Could his brother have brought his bride to a more desolate godforsaken place? Everywhere he looked, he saw things that needed fixed.

Before she ran him off, he'd repair all he could and make her life easier. He owed her that. Murmuring low curses, he pushed away from the post that held up the slanted roof of the porch and ambled toward the well.

A short while later, he sat down at the table with Skye. The meal was simple. He wasted no time filling his plate.

"How far is your closest neighbor?" he asked around a mouthful of food.

"Six miles thereabouts."

"And your nearest town?"

"Zapata is twenty miles. I only go every six months."

"Makes for a lonely life." Cade fought the urge to lean across the table and tuck a flame-colored tendril behind her ear. "How long since Matthew died?"

"Over five months ago. Why all the questions, Cade?"

He shrugged. "Want to get a feel for things is all."

"You won't be here long enough for that."

"I understand why you're angry and I don't blame you. This wild country is unforgiving. Lord knows you've given it your all. But why do you stay? Why not pack up?"

"And go where exactly? With what? I don't have anything but this god-blessed land and you can see men are lining up in droves to buy it."

"I apologize. Didn't mean to say you aren't trying."

She pushed back her chair and stalked from the house.

Cade ate the rest of the meal then went out to sit in the shade of the porch and regain his strength. He didn't know where Skye disappeared to. Clearly, showing up out of the blue this way had thrown her. Deep regret weighed him down. He'd close his eyes for just a moment then figure out where to start making amends.

But he didn't open them until the morning sun jarred him awake. He was still on her porch in the chair he'd dropped into. A light blanket covered him. He felt stronger. Getting to his feet, he noticed Skye working with the downed fence posts. He strode down to join her. He didn't like the rotten feeling in his gut.

"Who pulled these posts up?"

"I never said anyone did."

"Didn't have to. I've got eyes. Someone yanked these out of the ground deliberately."

"Stay out of it," she said sharply.

"Matthew would want me to help. Who did this?"

"Why, so you can kill him?"

Cade winced. "So I can fix the problem. That's what I do."

"Let it go, Cade. You can't always fight my battles."

"I can this one." He pulled her against him. "I'm not going to stand by and let anyone hurt you."

"Fine." Skye slumped as if all the air went out of her. "His name is Hiram Dunston."

Rage grew as she told him about Dunston trying to force himself on her and now he was bent on destroying her. It was only a matter of time before the man killed her.

"Where does he live?" Deadly calm underscored Cade's question.

"If I wanted to kill him, I'd have done that myself, Cade. I keep a loaded gun handy."

He brushed a finger along her delicate jawline. "I've never been one to turn the other cheek. Where does he live? I'll find out one way or the other."

"In Zapata. He's nothing but a drunk and a gambler. I can handle him."

"I can see that." He clenched his jaw. Watching someone bully a woman or child got to him quicker than rising flood waters on the Rio Grande. He'd deal with Dunston before he rode on. Men like Cade were good at that at least, if little else.

Taking the posthole digger from her, he gently pushed her toward the house. "Go do something easier. Make us some breakfast. I'll take care of this."

Cade removed his shirt and laid it aside, then tackled the job. He only stopped to eat. The sun beat down and sweat dripped off him. It felt good to use his hands, though, doing something meaningful. By the time the sun set, he had all the posts back in the ground and the wire restrung. He carried everything to the barn and washed up for supper then strode to the house.

Skye was dishing up red beans and cornbread. She turned when he entered. "Have a seat. I'm sure you worked up quite an appetite. I appreciate the help with the fence."

"I'll do more tomorrow."

She didn't mention his leaving as they ate. He guessed she wouldn't toss him out on his ear. Not yet.

"Mind if I borrow your horse tomorrow? I need to ride into town and see about getting another of my own. I'll pick up anything you need."

"You can use the horse. Don't get anything for me, though."

He laid his hand on hers and she didn't pull away. "If you had plenty of money what would you buy?"

* * *

Skye glanced down at his long, tanned fingers, remembering how they'd once caressed every inch of her body. Oft times, she'd remarked that he had a magical touch. Even now, a ribbon of pleasure spiraled down her spine.

Jerking her hand from beneath his, she spoke sharply, "This is a crazy game and …." She inhaled a calming breath. "I'll get you a blanket and you can sleep in the barn."

Cade got slowly to his feet and reached for his hat. "Didn't expect anything else."

Returning, she tossed him a blanket. When he closed the door behind him, she moved to the window. The purple and orange sunset outlined his figure. Tall and lean, he had a fluid unhurried walk, like a stream meandering along its course.

His corded forearms hung loosely at his side within easy reach of the Colt in his holster.

Cade Coltrain was a dangerous man. He'd always been someone to reckon with, but adding in the hardness that swept the length of him now he could put the fear of God in a man with only a single look. Violence was coiled inside him ready to unleash without warning.

In her heart, she knew the truth. He'd become a gunfighter and an outlaw who made his living killing people.

But, it didn't matter. Nothing did.

A sudden need to be held in those strong arms washed over her. She rested her head on the thick window pane and swallowed down the thick, bitter regret.

Finally, the loud ticking clock reminded her she had dishes to do. Raising her head, she brushed away her tears. Glancing out the window once more, she found Cade standing beside Matthew's grave with his head bowed.

What would he say to the brother who'd married the woman Cade had cast aside when adventure called?

She prayed he'd move on soon, before she gave in to the desire that created such a powerful ache in her body.

Oh, for once more to be held again, feel warm breath on her cheek; lay her palm on the hard muscles that rippled beneath the skin—make love until dawn. She couldn't put a price on those but they were the things she'd buy, if only she could.

Skye needed to be a woman again. Someone cherished.

~Chapter 3~

When Cade came in for breakfast before daybreak, Skye had stacked clean clothes neatly in his chair. He caught her glance and lifted an eyebrow in askance.

"You and Matthew wore about the same size. Put these on and I'll wash yours while you're in town."

"I appreciate that. They sure could stand freshening up. I've saddled your horse and will head out after I grab a cup of coffee."

"I've cooked eggs. You'll eat them."

He grinned. "Yes, ma'am. Anyone tell you you're bossy?"

"They didn't dare."

His heart turned over when she smiled back. He suspected she'd had no reason to smile in a long time, and was glad he could do that small thing for her.

Roughly two hours later, Cade rode into Zapata, Texas. He went straight to the livery. With luck, he could trade his services for a horse. The liveryman's eyes lit up when Cade inquired about work. He'd busted his leg and couldn't do more than hobble around on a crutch.

"I'll swap that four-year-old buckskin out in the corral and two dollars if you'll muck out the stalls and do odd jobs for me," the liveryman bargained.

"Seems more than a fair trade," Cade agreed.

After finishing, he collected the horse and his two dollars and went to the mercantile. No matter what Skye said, he knew she had needs. Selecting a smoked ham, he turned to the women's portion of the store. A pretty chemise made of soft linen caught his eye. He had the clerk wrap that up along with a nightgown of the finest cotton and set out for the homestead.

Though it took his last cent, he considered his purchases money well-spent.

* * *

With Cade gone, Skye hauled water from the well and got ready to do laundry. When she picked up his shirt, a gold locket with a broken chain fell out of the pocket. Curious, she pushed the clasp.

On one side was her image. Cade's sat opposite.

A wounded cry sprang from her mouth as she gripped the locket. Her heart beat wildly.

Memories came unbidden. He'd given it to her six years ago when they'd lain beneath the stars and dreamed of a life together. The broken chain was no surprise. When he'd told her he had some living to do and that he wouldn't settle down anytime soon, she'd been deeply hurt. But then when he added that she should marry his brother Matthew who'd been after her for months, that had utterly destroyed her.

In a fury, she'd ripped the locket from her neck and thrown it at his retreating backside.

Now, she clutched the necklace to her and allowed tears to fall, crying for the love she could never forget no matter how hard she tried.

A love she could never have.

A love he'd possibly given to another.

Yet, the keepsake evidently meant a lot to him. He'd kept it all this time, over the many miles he'd traveled. That was something, seeing as how he could number each of his worldly goods on one hand and have two fingers left over.

Stifling a sob, she laid it aside and sank into a chair, trying to understand why he'd kept the locket, trying to figure out what it meant.

* * *

Cade rode in just as the sun was setting. He was satisfied with his purchases, but disappointed that he hadn't gotten a chance to set Hiram Dunston straight. Folks told Cade he'd gotten stinkin' drunk and was in jail. His conversation with the rotten low-life would have to wait. He didn't like waiting.

Clothes flapped in the breeze on the line beside the house. Skye had been busy. He didn't see her anywhere and assumed she was inside. He led the horses to the small corral beside the barn, unsaddled hers, and turned both loose.

Thrusting a hand into his pocket for luck, sheer panic set in.

He'd lost the locket. His most cherished possession. Hurrying into the house, he stooped to look under the table and around the room. Movement drew him up short.

Skye stood with arms folded. "Looking for something?"

"You might say that I am. Something I greatly treasure that's brought me good luck."

"Would this be it, by chance?" She opened her hand and the gold locket dangled from a finger.

Cade swallowed hard, waiting for her anger. "You found it."

The lines of her face softened, surprising him. "Why did you keep it, Cade?"

"It reminded me of the price I paid for my own stupidity." He covered the space between them and took it. "And I never get tired of looking at your picture. Remembering. Dreaming."

"I didn't know you cared, didn't know that you gave me another thought after that day and the horrible words that were spoken."

He forced out the words he'd locked in a far corner of his heart. "I cared. Always."

Slowly, he moved closer until only a whisper of distance remained between them. He caressed her cheek with the back of his fingers. "You don't know what you do to a man. You're impossible to forget."

Skye leaned into him. "What did we do, Cade? I loved you, you know."

"But Matthew—"

"Matthew wasn't *you*. He was a good husband, but I never loved him. I only gave my heart away once … and you gave it back."

"I was a fool." His ragged breath was loud in his ears. Familiar heat pooled low in his belly. He bent his head and crushed his lips to hers.

* * *

Skye closed her eyes. Like the brush of fine silk, the sweep of his mouth across hers stole her breath, her thoughts, and any desire to resist.

An overpowering hunger rose up.

But what would happen when he rode off again without looking back? Could she keep it from destroying her?

She pushed away from his broad chest and stumbled outside. The old dugout drew her, the place she always sought when life pressed around crushing her. She sank into the chair she'd put there long ago and buried her face in her hands.

The lines had blurred and she didn't know how that happened. Cade Coltrain was no longer her husband's brother. He was her love. And God knew if he kissed her again, she'd lose all ability to resist.

Even if he made no promise to stay she would welcome the warmth of his arms.

Purple twilight cast deep shadows before she returned to the house. She busied herself bringing in the clothes and folding them, cooking a meal. Once she spied the smoked ham on the table, supper was easy.

The package wrapped in brown paper sitting next to the ham aroused her curiosity. She rested her hand on it.

Whistling, Cade strolled through the door. "Open it."

"I told you I didn't want anything."

"But you never said a word about *need*." Cade's blue eyes were as soft as his words.

"The money used to buy these things—"

"Was come by honest," he finished. "Worked at the livery in exchange for the buckskin and two dollars. So don't stand there. Open it."

Tearing away the paper her breath caught in her throat. "Oh, Cade!"

The chemise was lovely with its lace and pretty pink ribbon. She held it up to her for a second before turning to the nightgown in the paper. She ran her fingers across the fabric, admiring the tiny pink rosettes sewn around the neck and sleeves. Simply beautiful—and much needed.

"I thought you'd like them," Cade said quietly.

"No one ever bought me anything like this." She laid her gifts down. "Your peace offering?"

"No. My reason is simple. I saw them and thought they might put a smile on that pretty face of yours. Nothing more, nothing less. You have every right to your anger. Hold on to it, Skye. At least you're feeling something. Helps you remember you're not dead."

"I want to be sometimes when life stomps on me." She put the gifts away and sliced some of the ham then opened her last jar of fresh peas. She also found a can of peaches for dessert.

Sitting across from him, she brought up the subject she'd been dreading. "Did you find Dunston in town?"

"Nope." His eyes met hers. "You can relax. The louse is in jail. I still mean to have a talk with him before I leave though."

"I wish you'd drop it."

"Not a chance."

After supper, Cade disappeared outside while she washed the dishes. Probably doing some last minute chores before turning in. She rigged a blanket to separate the kitchen from the rest of the house. Dragging in her washtub, she filled it with water. She wanted to be clean when she put on the new nightgown. Her bath didn't take long and when she came out, Cade sat at the table.

Still wet, his hair curled around the neck of his clean shirt. He smiled. "Looks like we both had the same idea. Not much water in the pitiful little creek I found behind the house but it was enough. The gown looks real pretty on you, Skye."

75

"Thank you again for it."

He unwound his long legs and stood. "I'll empty the tub."

"I appreciate that." The bed against the wall drew her attention. Something rested on the pillow.

Curiosity was so strong she barely heard Cade carry the tub outside. She moved slowly to the bed. A perfectly shaped heart made from a piece of leather lay on her pillow. A thin strip of red fabric was woven around the outer edge, and colorful feathers filled the center. Her breath caught as she picked it up and stroked the small gift.

Cade opened the door and stepped inside. "Not my best work."

"It's just lovely. Did you make it?"

"Yeah, not a very good job, I'm afraid. Didn't have a lot to work with. The leather came from a flap of my saddlebags. The rest, I found in town today. Do you like it?"

"I love it." Skye laid it down. "Cade, will you hold me?"

He moved to her and she melted in his arms, breathing his clean fragrance. His light touch on the back of her head, his gentle breath ruffling the hair at her temple, and his strong heartbeat beneath her ear renewed her sagging spirit.

Skye glanced up. "Do you think you could sleep inside the house tonight? I'm lonely."

Instead of a reply, he swept her into his arms and carried her to the bed. "Anything to ease your loneliness, pretty lady. Just let me blow out the lamps."

When darkness filled the room, he sat on the side of the bed, undid his holster, and pulled his boots off. Then she heard him getting out of the rest of his clothes. She wished the lamp still burned so she could see his muscular body. It had been so long.

He stretched out beside her and pulled her close. His tender touch on her body after so long was almost more than she could bear. Tears bubbled in her eyes. This man who wanted to protect her and had fashioned a heart from a piece of leather from his saddlebags was unaware of the true gift he gave her.

She rose long enough to pull her nightgown over her head then she nestled in his strong arms.

The kiss they shared spoke of need and passion. And a deep hunger to matter to someone.

~Chapter 4~

Moonlight filtered in through the window illuminating the beautiful woman lying next to him.

Cade rose on an elbow and trailed feathery kisses across Skye's eyelids, her delicate cheekbones, and down the slender curve of her throat. Though she tried to pull him on top of her, he would have none of it. He meant to enjoy every second of their fleeting time.

He slid a lazy hand up her long, shapely legs and left dawdling caresses along their length.

"Turn on your belly, darlin'," he said.

When she obeyed, he slid his palm down the curve of her spine to her firm bottom. A moan slid from her lips as he moved her hair aside and feathered kisses from the back of her neck down her sleek body.

Each touch awakened a hundred treasured memories of time spent loving her. A life he'd thrown away to chase a fickle dream.

"That's enough." Skye turned back over and tugged at him. "I need you, Cade. Now."

"Not yet." He stared down, his gaze worshiping her. Skye's breath became ragged as she stroked his chest and back.

Her velvet skin was silkier than he remembered. He moved lower, kissing and caressing every inch.

Returning to her mouth, he whispered roughly, "You are the most incredible woman I've ever known, Skye O'Rourke. I'd give anything to spend the rest of my days with you."

Her hand seared a path across the corded muscles of his chest. "Shhhh. All we have for sure is right now, this moment. Maybe we don't have a right to ask for more."

Cade tenderly smoothed back her hair and wiped away the tears that leaked from the corner of her eyes.

When he could bear no more sweet torment, he positioned himself on top of her and took all that she wanted to give.

The pleasure was almost more than he could bear and when release came, he could've sworn all his bones turned to liquid.

How could he tell Skye how much he still loved her?

Yet, what right did he have to speak of such things? He'd given her to his brother.

Fool!

Long after their bodies had cooled and sleep claimed Skye, Cade lay listening to her soft breathing and counted himself a very lucky man.

For what she'd just given him, he'd crawl naked over a thorny field under a scorching sun. Skye was his one true love and always would be, until a bullet found him and ended his torment.

* * *

Over the next week, Cade worked making repairs and fixing things. But when night fell, Skye welcomed him into her bed. She dreaded the day when he'd ride out, chasing his next adventure.

How would she go back to her empty life? How could she forget the sound of the male rumble in his chest when he kissed her? And how could she forget their lovemaking that was sometimes slow and passionate and other times raw and frenzied? She told herself not to get too attached to him.

But her heart refused to listen.

A little over a week since his arrival, Skye woke to find her milk cow dead with an arrow protruding from the heifer's neck and belly. Cold fear spread down her spine and along her nerve endings.

Cade pulled out the arrow and broke it over his knee. Silently, his searching gaze swept the land around the homestead. "Go in the house, Skye," he said quietly.

She wasted no time arguing. Hurrying into the house, she bolted the door and reached for her rifle. Despite the arrow, she knew who was to blame. Hiram Dunston couldn't fool her. But Cade was here now. He wouldn't let Dunston hurt her.

Unless he caught Cade by surprise and killed him.

Quaking inside, her breath stilled as she listened for sounds beyond her door.

Time seemed to stand still. At last, Cade hollered to let him in. She threw the bolt and hugged him.

"I dragged the cow a good distance down to a ravine."

"I've never known Dunston to use arrows before," Skye said. "Do you think—"

81

"It was him all right."

"Did you see him?"

"No. But hoof prints around the cow were the exact same as the prints near the fence posts he yanked from the ground."

The day wore on with no sign of Dunston. Skye relaxed. Maybe he went back to town. The man could've seen Cade and decided things were too dangerous for him. She hoped so.

Still, what would happen when Cade left? Cold knowledge washed over her. Either she would kill Dunston—or he'd kill her. She knew that as sure as the sun rose.

For supper that night, she fixed a stew from her limited larder and made cornbread. Cade talked about some of his travels. He'd been all the way to California, Montana and up in the Dakotas.

"Hid out for a while in the Badlands of South Dakota. Posse chased me to hell and back."

"Why?"

"A big rancher I'd worked for got murdered. They claimed I did it."

Skye placed her hand over Cade's. Her question was soft. "If you were innocent, why didn't you tell them and clear your name?"

He snorted. "They weren't exactly in the mood to talk. They'd have hung me first thing from the highest tree and asked questions later. Men live by a different set of rules up there. But there were plenty of men I did put in a grave, so I guess it sort of evens out in the end."

"No wonder you dodged my question about being wanted."

"My name's on a poster in most states, even Texas," he admitted. "Let's talk about other things. How did Matthew die? You never said."

Skye worried with the edge of her apron remembering that awful day. "Horse stepped in a hole and fell. Matthew landed beneath the animal and died instantly."

"At least he went fast. Did you have a good life with him before …?"

She sighed, choosing her words carefully. "Matthew did his best. You can't make yourself love someone if the feelings aren't there."

"I can relate to that. Is it too late to start over, pretend I didn't hurt you?"

How could they begin again when he meant to ride off at the first opportunity? Sudden thickness in her throat made it difficult to swallow. She rose to clear the table.

It was strange how much of her life she'd spent in denial and pretense. She'd pretended not to care when Cade left, pretended to love Matthew, pretended she hadn't had to marry to save her reputation.

But the greatest lie she told herself was that she had only carried Cade's child a few short months.

~Chapter 5~

Cade strapped on his Colt and saddled his buckskin early the next morning. He needed to ride, sort things out. That Skye hadn't answered his question about starting over chewed on him like a rabid dog.

In his heart, he knew she could never pretend he hadn't hurt her. That kind of pain went bone deep. Forgiving time was past.

She didn't trust him.

Hell, he didn't trust himself. He knew he could never settle down and live here. The life of a farmer wasn't for him.

Not even the deep abiding love he felt for Skye could put a plow in his hand and attachment for this godforsaken land in his blood.

What had drawn his older brother to this rough terrain?

Much lay untouched, left to the thorny brush and cacti. The wild rugged expanse stretched as far as the eye could see.

Skimming the ground, feeling the horse's powerful muscles beneath him, brought some sense of peace.

He'd just reined the buckskin in when his stomach clenched tight making it hard to breathe.

Trouble rode the wind.

Trouble he couldn't ignore.

Skye was in danger. He knew it as sure as he knew his name.

* * *

Humming, Skye opened the chicken coop Cade had built and stepped inside. She gathered the eggs and took them to the house where she set them on the table.

Her heart was light for the first time in a long while. Lying in Cade's strong arms each night, touching his body and having him touch her had brought a sense of well-being.

But it was a false sense of security.

Cade didn't belong in this world. He was a dreamer and a wanderer who lived by the gun.

Unconsciously, her hand drifted to her stomach where perhaps a new life already grew. A child would lessen the loneliness and make it easier to face each new sunrise. She'd give it all the love she possessed.

Just as she turned to tackle the rest of her chores, a hand closed around her throat.

"You belong to me, woman. Time for a little fun." The deep raspy voice filled the small dwelling, settling into the corners. "I came to get my due. I won't leave less'n I get it."

Skye's blood froze in her veins. Her thoughts had been so firmly on Cade she'd forgotten to watch out for snakes under her feet. A hurried glance found her rifle leaning against the wall—too far away.

Shaking, she slowly swiveled and stared into Hiram Dunston's ugly pockmarked face. "Then get ready to die. My husband's brother will be back any second. He'll give you everything you're due and then some."

"No one wants you. You're used up," he snarled.

"Begs the question—why are *you* here?"

"I ain't too particular and I like a wildcat."

"My husband's brother is a wanted man and it won't bother him to kill one more." Her breath came in great heaving gasps. She stomped his feet, pounded his chest, clawed his face. Doing whatever she could to free herself.

Dunston whipped a gun from his waistband and pressed the cold steel to her forehead. "You're lyin', tryin' to save your own skin."

"Then you're surely a fool," she said softly.

He jerked her against him by her hair. "Only one man called me a fool. He's dead."

With a curse, he slung her across the room, laughed when she landed on the floor, slamming her head against the iron bedstead. Though pain shot through her body, she refused to utter a sound.

"Now, get those clothes off before I lose my patience." Laying his pistol on the table, he crept slowly toward her.

It took all her strength to pull herself to her feet. Her fingers trembled so badly she had trouble getting the small buttons through the holes. With no weapons within reach, she steeled herself for what was to come.

"Quit stalling, woman. Ain't no one gonna save you. Make no mistake about it, I'll take what's mine come hell or high water."

The door suddenly burst open and slammed back against the wall. Cade stood with his Colt drawn in the opening, his feet braced widely apart. The lines of his face had hardened into a mask.

Dunston whirled, his tongue working in his mouth. "What do you want, mister?"

Without answering, Cade moved from the doorway, positioning himself between the attacker and his gun. Skye could see his steely calm despite the rage that darkened his eyes.

"Who are you, mister?"

"I am your hell and high water," Cade thundered. "One twitch and you're dead."

All color drained from Dunston's face, leaving it ashen. His Adam's apple bobbed when he swallowed hard. "I ain't done nothing. No crime agin visitin' the widow. Who did you say you are?"

"A man you don't want to mess with. I promise you won't like the result." Cade's blue eyes swept to Skye where she clutched her partially unbuttoned dress. The muscles worked in his jaw. She knew Dunston lived on borrowed time.

"I'll share the woman if that's what you want. Even let you go first." As Dunston spoke, he made a sudden move to his boot and jerked out a derringer.

Cade pulled the trigger of his Colt. Orange flame and smoke shot from the barrel. The bullet slammed into Dunston's chest, propelling him backward where he sank to the floor in a pool of blood.

Trembling, Skye rose and threw her arms around Cade. "I was afraid you wouldn't return before he …"

* * *

"Shhhh." He held her tight, burying his face in her pretty red hair. "I'm here now, darlin', and he's dead. He'll never bother you again."

"I was terrified."

"So was I," he admitted.

"Now what? What are we going to do with him? They'll hang you." Her stricken gaze met his. "Run. Get far away from here. I'll cover for you."

"One thing you should know about me. I don't run." Cade smoothed her hair. "I'm not leaving you again. If I go, you're coming."

Skye glanced around the dwelling. "There's nothing here for me."

"Gather whatever belongings you want that'll fit on a horse. I'm taking you far away from here. I love you, Skye."

She laid a hand on his jaw. "There was never a time when I didn't love you. I won't lie and say you didn't hurt me, but I can forgive you. You have my heart."

"I'll protect it with my life this time." He kissed her fingers.

An hour later, Cade set fire to the house and the monster inside. He watched the flames glowing in the window, saw the roof catch.

Strolling up from behind, he slid his arms around Skye's waist. "Any regrets?"

"None. I expected sadness, but it didn't come. Instead, I realized that this is the finality of one part of my life and I've just begun a new chapter. I can't wait to see how this book reads."

"I intend to spend the rest of my life showing you all the ways I love you. Where do you want to go, Mrs. Coltrain?"

"Anywhere you are. We've waited a long time to be together. This is a wild untamed land with plenty of places to dream and work and raise a family."

He pressed a kiss to her temple, his chest swelling in gratitude for the woman who held his heart. "I know of an old trapper's cabin hidden way back in the Colorado Rockies. I wintered there quite a bit. No one will bother us. The land is good and fertile and there's a beautiful stream filled with trout next to the cabin. We can go there."

Laying her palm on the side of his face, she met his gaze. "It sounds like pure heaven, sweetheart."

"Nothing will ever come between us again. I won't give you one reason for regret. The love I saved for you is the lasting kind." He brought her hand to his mouth and kissed her fingertips. "I'm taking off my gun and picking up a plow."

Skye's gray eyes darkened. "I'll never ask you to change, not for me."

"I know."

"To work, it has to be because you want to and no other." She leaned against him and plucked a loose string from his shirt. Her stern voice held a warning. "When I marry you, it'll be for the rest of my life so don't go thinking it's only temporary. It's not."

Cade grinned. "All right then. I guess it's settled. We'd best get moving."

With love bursting from his heart, he made a step with his hands and helped her onto her horse. Without a backward glance, they set out with hope toward a bright future. No longer would his beautiful Skye be sad and alone. He'd see to that.

Love could build a bridge between yesterday and tomorrow.

Sometimes a man did get a second chance. This time he wouldn't squander it.

HARD LUCK

~Part One~

Texas Panhandle 1880

The plan sounded moderately safe—for the most part—yet unease gnawed in his stomach with sharp, tiny rat-teeth, looking for a way out.

Logan Bartee jumped from his chair and strode to look out the window at the Texas landscape. The panhandle held the type of stark beauty that had to grow on a man, but once it did he couldn't leave. He loved it here so why was he trying to mess that up?

Friendship for one. And a life debt for another.

"It'll be as easy as taking candy from a baby."

Wade 'Catfish' George, a man three years younger than Logan's twenty-eight, glanced up from his crude sketch of Hard Luck, Texas. He scratched his ear with a pinky finger and forced a grin. "There's no law, no one to worry about. Shoot, half the people don't even wear a gun."

"Wade, whenever something looks too good to be true, it's best to run." Logan released a worried sigh, wishing like hell he could walk away.

Only he was bound tight. He wouldn't be alive if not for Wade after he was bitten by a deadly copperhead a year ago. As it was, Logan had come near to losing his damn hand and still wore a painful reminder. Wade found him near death and hauled him forty miles in a blinding sandstorm to the nearest doctor. But all that aside, they'd been best friends since kids. Yep, he owed the man whose parents added Catfish to Wade's name and made him the butt of jokes.

Logan turned from the window. "Maybe you could beg the bank president for mercy and ask for more time. I'll help you raise the money to keep your farm—the right way."

"I already tried that, Logan. That stuffed scarecrow Snodgrass set the deadline a week from today, no exceptions. And you've already given me all you can spare. I can't lose the only thing my daddy ever gave me. We're in a drought and nothing will grow in this dry, godforsaken dirt without rain." Wade's voice dropped as though ashamed to say the words. "You owe me, Logan."

Hell, it wasn't as if Logan had forgotten. Although he pondered the fact he must have manure for brains, he hadn't become senile. He went back to the table and sat down, stretching out his long legs in front of him.

"I've already been and watched their routine," Wade went on, giving his unkept sandy hair an impatient shove. "It's the same every dadgum day. The best time to rob the bank is right before closing. No customers will be there and the teller won't pay us any mind 'cause he'll be getting' ready to go home. Hard Luck is a sleepy little town." Wade rubbed the back of his neck. "We'll ride in and out before they even know we're there."

Logan's eyes narrowed. "And what if things turn sideways?"

"Heck, if there was some other way, don't you think I'd take it?" A nervous tic developed in Wade's left eye.

A million things could go wrong. At least Wade had sense enough to realize what they faced—jail being one of them. Hell! The chewing in Logan's gut got worse.

Just let him get through this in one piece and he'd never break the law again. That's all he asked.

* * *

Late the next afternoon, they reined up on a hill above Hard Luck. Even from a distance, Logan could tell they'd given it the right name. The town had nothing to recommend it. The buildings that still stood sagged and in bad need of whitewash and the few citizens moved about as though in a daze.

Hard luck was beyond sleepy, it was snoring painfully loud.

"Well?" Wade asked.

"It doesn't appear to pose too many problems. But let's get this clear. I help you and we're done being outlaws." Logan leaned his elbow on the pommel and fixed Wade with a hard stare. "No matter how much there is, you take what you need and leave the rest. Understood?"

"Of course. It's not like I want to make this my life's profession. You know what drove me here. The blame lies with old man Snodgrass."

No, the blame was two-fold—the weather and Wade's shortsightedness. He didn't follow Logan's example and sell off most of his herd when the drought hit or dig a water well. It would be tough but Logan would survive until the rains came. Wade wouldn't.

"Stop blaming Snodgrass," Logan snapped. The hot sun bore down making him grouchier than usual. "And he's not that old."

"It wouldn't be any skin off his nose to give me a few extra months," Wade said a mite defensive.

Resigned, Logan asked, "What's your brilliant plan? Do we cover our faces?"

Wade snorted. "Now that would be plumb stupid to stroll into the bank that way. The teller would know right away we're there to rob the place and go for his gun before we even get through the door. We walk in like normal people."

"Thought you said we didn't have to worry about guns."

"Well, I'm sure it's safe to assume a teller would have one. How else would he guard the money—stick out his finger and threaten to shoot?"

"Whatever you say. I'm just here to keep you from getting your head blown off." Logan tugged on the reins and pointed the horse toward town. "Let's get this over with."

Halfway down the hill, Wade's flea-bitten piebald stepped into a hole and developed a bad limp which called for walking into Hard Luck afoot, leading the horses down the main street. The town's curse appeared to have already struck. A sign they shouldn't ignore.

Logan pushed back his worn hat, scanning the sorry-looking buildings. "Look, Wade, we don't have to go through with this. You won't even be able to make a quick getaway. We can get us a cold beer at the saloon and go back home."

"What's got into you?" Wade stared at Logan like he'd just called his mother a nasty name. "Rooster will be fine. He just needs to rest that leg a bit."

"Whatever you say." And who named his horse Rooster?

Wade huffed. "Well, he's my damn horse and if I say he's fine, he's good."

They meandered past the row of leaning, unpainted establishments. It boggled Logan's mind how they even had a bank to begin with. The thing couldn't have much money in it.

As they moved toward a saloon that didn't even have a name, Wade said, "As long as we're here, we might as well have a beer. We have some time to kill before we go to the bank."

One more chance to talk him out of it. Logan glanced at the hitching rail laying on the ground. Wade acted as if that was normal. Without a word, he bent and poked the reins underneath the post. Logan shook his head and followed suit.

The barkeep was sound asleep, his head on the bar. Logan pounded on the splintered wooden plank.

The man jerked awake. "Uh ....what can I get you?"

"Two beers." Logan fished two bits from his pocket and pitched it on the bar. He glanced at the cracked mirror in front of him. He and Wade *appeared* two ordinary, reasonably smart cowboys. Not simple at all. Hardworking too with their lives in front of them. Logan's dark hair and square jaw that sported two days' worth of whiskers had been known to turn a woman's head. Too bad he wasn't much in the brain department or he wouldn't be there.

The barkeep filled two chipped mugs and set them down. Grabbing the quarter, he put the edge in his mouth and bit down. Satisfied it was real, he dropped it in the till.

The beer was hot. Logan hated hot beer. At the sound of sobs, he glanced around and noticed a man in a dark corner, weeping his heart out. Logan met Wade's glance and shrugged his shoulders.

"Hey, mister, what's wrong with that man?" Wade asked the bartender.

"His favorite settin' hen up and died, horse ran off, house burned, and his wife left with the fat man in the circus." The barkeep knocked a scorpion from the plank. "Ain't nothin' but bad luck in this town. If'n I was you, I'd get on my horse, if he's still alive, and ride like hell."

"See what I told you, Wade? Let's go." Logan downed his beer and stood, plunking down the empty mug.

Wade hurried after him. "Now hold up there, Logan. I ain't done."

Outside, Logan confronted him, towering over his friend by two inches. "I am."

"You owe me," Wade said in a hoarse whisper. "Just help me this once. That's all and we'll call it even."

Logan stood there for a minute. "Dammit!" Leaning, he yanked the horse's reins from under the hitching rail. "Come on."

They walked to the bank and secured the horses, then sauntered inside.

The teller, a balding man around forty or so, was scribbling something in a ledger. He didn't glance up.

Wade stood there in silence, shifting his weight back and forth. Logan was happy to note that the bank was empty of customers, but through a crack in the door behind the teller, he saw a man sitting at a desk. The bank president?

The rat-teeth gnawed through Logan's stomach and crawled up his spine.

"Excuse me," Wade finally said, drawing his pistol. He stuck it through the iron bars at the teller. "This is a hold up. Give me one hundred and ninety-eight dollars and sixty-two cents."

The teller jerked back and barked, "No."

"No? Maybe you can't see this gun." Wade's face flushed as he waved the pistol. "I'm making a withdrawal."

"No. I can't give it to you or I'll be fired. Do you know how impossible it is to get a job in Hard Luck?" the teller asked.

Logan stepped forward. "Look, we're sorry. We understand, but we wouldn't be here if we didn't need to be. Just hand over the money and we'll be gone."

The door flew open and a woman with a rather large belly rushed inside. "Help me, I'm having my baby. I … I don't know what to do." She clutched Logan's arm. "I need help."

What gave her the idea that Logan knew about such things was beyond him. He glanced around and spied a dusty sofa in the corner. "The first thing you need to do is get off your feet."

With Wade still holding the gun on the teller, Logan helped the young woman to the sofa.

Panting and moaning and carrying on, she stretched out. "I'm so hot."

"Maybe you should ... uh ... loosen your collar," he suggested, shooting Wade a dark scowl. "Is there a doctor in town?"

"He left three years ago," the teller said helpfully with his hands raised.

The bank president rushed from his office, smoking a cigar. "What's going on out here?"

"We're being robbed," the teller provided. "And Martha Ann is having a baby."

"Good Lord!" The bank owner turned green, laying his cigar on a piece of wooden molding. He turned to Wade, "Put down that gun, shorty, or you'll shoot someone. We have no money to rob."

Wade's jaw jutted out. "Every bank has money." He poked the gun into the tubby man's belly. "Open your safe and we'll be on our way."

Logan knelt beside Martha Ann and patted her hand. He watched Wade and the bank president disappear into a little airless cubicle. What was he supposed to do now? On his ranch, he just hooked a rope to the calf's legs and pulled but something said Martha Ann wouldn't like that much. Besides, the heifers never wore a dress and fourteen thousand petticoats and other items of clothing.

Water, he needed water.

Before he could ask the teller where to find some, another woman rushed through the door, followed by a parade of people. The small bank quickly filled up, taking all the air.

The woman leading the charge knelt beside Logan. She gave him a brilliant smile that lit up her blue eyes. "Thank you so much for helping Martha Ann. You must be her husband that we've been expecting. I'm Susan. It's a pleasure to meet you."

"Likewise," Logan muttered in shock. "I'm not her ... we're not ... she's not ..."

Just then Martha Ann let out a bloodcurdling scream and squeezed Logan's hand until tears came into his eyes. The woman was sure strong. Once he freed himself, he stood. "Look, folks, can you give Martha Ann some privacy here?"

The explosion of a gunshot deafened Logan. What in the hell had Wade done? Pulling his old Colt Paterson, Logan rushed past the wide-eyed teller curled in a ball on the floor of the teller's cage and into the cubicle. The bank president held a smoking gun and Wade clutched his foot, his face white. Through the smoke, Logan noticed the safe standing wide open and it was clearly empty. Not one single coin in it.

Logan barked, "Put down the pistol, mister."

Tension crackled in the air like lightning striking a weathervane and his heartbeat thundered in his ears. Indecision rippled in the man's eyes.

Finally, the bank owner complied, laying the weapon on the floor. "It went off accidentally. I didn't mean to shoot him—although I was certainly within my rights."

Keeping his Colt on the man, Logan put an arm around Wade. "We're getting the hell out of here and I don't want to hear a word."

They rushed from the establishment to the horses. Rooster laid on the ground. The piebald lifted his head and looked at them. Wade knelt to try to cajole the animal into getting up but had no luck.

"Get on my horse. We'll ride double." Logan kept a firm grip on his friend to prevent him from collapsing beside old Rooster. He boosted Wade up behind the saddle then mounted. Bullets peppered the ground as the horse leapt into a gallop and soon left the town of Hard Luck in their dust.

"My Rooster," Wade bellowed. "I can't leave him like this. He's all I got."

Linda Broday

They rode for about a mile before cutting down into a ravine out of sight. Best Logan could tell, no one followed. He dismounted and Wade slid from the back, dropping in the dirt, clutching his foot.

"Let me see." Logan squatted beside his friend. He wanted to yell and say I told you so, but now wasn't the time. He pulled off Wade's boot. The bullet had only grazed the top of his foot. "You're lucky."

"I don't know how you figure that. I'm shot, got a hole in my boot, my damn horse is sick, I ain't got any money to pay the bank, and I'm a wanted outlaw." Wade wasn't whining but awful close to it.

A grin flirted with the corner of Logan Bartee's mouth as he wrapped a bandana around the wound. "You're alive, aren't you? That's something, all considering. And they can't get you for bank robbery since there wasn't nothing in it to take. You're young enough to start over."

Wade squinted at him. "I won't ever go back to Hard Luck as long as I live. Hey, Logan, we could try another town—like Petunia or Loveland. Those sound safe."

"No!" Logan rose and strode to his horse that had moved to a few sprigs of wild grass.

"I'll bet we'd have better luck in Buttercup." Wade limped after him.

"No!"

"How about Sweet Springs?" Wade asked. "No bad luck there."

Logan helped him onto the roan then rested a hand on the saddle. "Stop or I'll stuff your boot in your mouth. I'm done. No more bank robbing for me. If you decide to try again, count me out. That back there was the last straw. I owe you more than I can ever repay but no more crime. I'll help you in any other way."

He climbed into the saddle and they rode along in silence for a spell. It was nice listening to the hawk soaring overhead and the roan snorting.

"Thank you, Logan," Wade said, ruining the quiet. "You've got a lot more smarts than I do. I sure thought that bank owner was going to kill me when he opened the safe and whipped out that gun. I was almost afraid to look down, expectin' to see my whole foot shot off. That town really had a powerful lot of bad luck."

"Crime doesn't pay. Let that be a lesson to you."

The West Texas wind blew through the short grass and juniper dotting the landscape. Logan relaxed, soaking up the sight he loved.

"Hey, I just had an idea!" Wade exclaimed. "There's a dance coming up in town and the women are raffling off the bachelors for Valentine's Day. I won't be able to waltz with my hurt foot but I can shuffle. How about we try that? Between you and me we could get the money for Snodgrass. We're both handsome and the ladies seem to like us—uh, you more than me—but I reckon I carry my own. This plan will sure enough work"

Logan rolled his eyes as Wade continued, the words coming faster than bullets from a Gatlin Gun.

"Still, I guess you'll probably bring in the most. It's easy. Nothing can go wrong. This time, it *will* be like taking candy from a baby. I promise. We just stand there, smile real big and wink. They'll love us. I think my middle name has something to do with the ladies refusing to let me court 'em. I can't think of any other reason. I'm nice and polite and have an irresistible grin that brings out the cleft in my chin. What do you think about my idea? You can ponder it for a bit before you decide."

"I can't hear you. I'm asleep," Logan growled.

~Part Two~

"Now tell me again how this is supposed to work?" Logan gave Wade his best scowl. Something told him that it wouldn't turn out any better than robbing the bank. "We get raffled off to the highest bidder and then what? *We* don't get the money. You know that, don't you?"

Wade snorted. "How dumb do you think I am?"

Well, pretty damn dumb to Logan's way of thinking. But despite that, he was a good friend.

Logan got up to refill their coffee cups. "You tell me. Sometimes things tend to get lost between your mouth and your brain."

"That's not so." Wade swelled up. "If you don't want to do this, just say so." He paused and leaned close, stabbing his finger on the table. "But you owe me."

There it was—the pity card. Wade wasn't going to let him forget.

He blew out an exasperated breath. "Back to the raffle and dance. Focus."

"We need two rich women to buy us and we'll work our charm. They'll open up their pocketbooks to us."

Rich women? In Coyote Springs? Fat chance. "How many single rich women do you know, Wade?"

"Well there's ... uh well." His friend frowned. "Just because I cain't recall doesn't mean they're not any."

"So, they're hiding?"

"Maybe."

"Let's say two rich ladies show up. How do you think we'll get them to bid on us?"

"We'll have to make sure they do, that's all. We will be the most handsome ones there. Have you looked at our competition? One has buck teeth, one losing his hair, and one as big around as a fish barrel." Wade died laughing.

Logan didn't see the humor. All he saw was trouble with a capital T. "If I do this, we're even. Got that? I never want to hear again how I owe you."

"Oh sure. We'll be square. As soon as I have the money to pay the bank."

"No. Not when you get money, not when you satisfy Mr. Snodgrass, and not when you decide the debt is paid. This is the last damn time."

"All right. You don't have to get so huffy about it."

"I'm also going to be the one in charge." Logan gave his friend a side glance. So far, Wade held his anger in check but then he really had no choice in the matter. He knew Logan would back out faster than he could spit.

Wade huffed. "Why all the rules? I never thought you wouldn't be in charge."

"Grab your hat. We're going to buy you some new clothes and then I'm giving you lessons on how to talk proper to a lady."

"I know how to do that!"

"Trust me, you don't." Logan got his hat and they rode into town.

Colorful banners hung across the dirt street advertising the Valentine's Day raffle and dance. They tied up at the hitching post and strolled into the mercantile. Twenty minutes later, they emerged with packages under their arms.

Now the real work would begin and Logan had no idea how to make a silk purse out of an ugly old sow's ear.

* * *

A week later, as twilight fell they rode up to the platform on Main Street and dismounted. The ladies of the Garden Club were putting finishing touches on the decorations. A bad feeling rumbled in Logan's gut. This wasn't going to turn out well.

"Now, remember to smile and swallow all your bellyaching no matter who wins you in the raffle," Logan lectured. "Dance with her and show her a good time. Understand?"

"I'm not exactly stupid, Logan."

Maybe not but then again, Wade definitely wasn't in line when the good Lord handed out brains. However, he'd proved to be his best friend all these years.

Folks jostled for a place near the stage. Logan herded Wade into a line with the other bachelors.

Pretty Cali Rose rested her arms on the stage and smiled up at Logan. "I have a whole two dollars and I'm wagering it all on you."

He squatted down to give her a kiss and the scent of roses wafted around him. He could see himself settling down with Cali Rose and having a mess of kids. She was the only woman in town he'd ever wanted to be with. "We'll have a good time, darlin'."

Soon the front rows were packed with single women and they appeared anxious for the bidding to begin. The cross-eyed barber was the first to step onto the auction block. A heavyset woman won him with a mere fifteen cents. One by one they all went off with their women partners for the dance.

Then it was Wade's turn. He stepped forward with a wide smile for the ladies in the front row. He turned to the left with his arm bent to reveal a muscle, then to the right as though showing himself off. A thin, reed-like woman offered a nickel and the bidding war grew with the amount reaching fifty cents.

Suddenly, a woman near the back stood and called out, "One dollar."

Logan craned his neck to see who the voice belonged to but she was in the shadows.

"We have one dollar. Who'll make it one dollar and ten cents?" the auctioneer asked.

No one spoke. The lady auctioneer banged her gavel. "The lady in the back has Wade Catfish George for the evening."

Wade's eyes were large and he swallowed hard as the thin woman came to claim him. She had her hair pulled back in a severe knot on the back of her neck and she wore a thick shawl that she clutched to her.

Well, it could've been worse, but Wade's frown showed bitter disappointment.

Logan was dead last. He moved into place. Cali Rose's hair glistened like pure gold in the lamplight as she fidgeted in her chair. He didn't think he'd ever seen a more beautiful woman. Or kinder.

Cali Rose was the one he was going to marry. She just didn't know it yet.

The bidding commenced but soon became a war between Cali Rose and the Widow Harvey. He didn't even know her first name, but she seemed desperate, going toe to toe with her opponent. Although she had nice eyes and pretty smile, he'd heard she had a mess of kids. Maybe she needed some work done around her place. That he could and would do no questions asked, but the widow had best not have courtship in mind or she'd be sorely disappointed.

The last tally was one dollar and fifty-five cents. Cali Rose only had two dollars.

Sweat rose on Logan's forehead. Why had he let Wade talk him into this?

"Do I hear two dollars?" the woman in charge asked. "Who'll give me two dollars for Logan Bartee? He's one fine specimen of a man with a heart of gold to match."

"Two dollars," Cali Rose cried.

Logan held his breath. The silence stretched for what seemed an eternity. He couldn't bear to glance at the Widow Harvey, staring at the back and the darkness that stretched beyond.

The auctioneer asked again. Still nothing.

A fly buzzed around Logan's head but he didn't shoo it away.

He stood frozen.

Waiting.

The pounding gavel made him flinch.

Cali Rose rushed forward. "I did it, Logan. I'll pay my money and we'll dance."

"I'll wait by the punchbowl."

She disappeared and Logan wandered toward the refreshment table.

Wade caught his arm and dragged him to the side. "I can't do this, Logan. I can't spend the evening with Mazie Snodgrass. Of all people to win me."

"What's wrong with her? Mazie seems pleasant enough." He glanced at her standing all alone, clutching her shawl. She tried not to show her disappointment but tears filled her pretty green eyes.

"She's not rich. She can't help me keep my land." He let out a loud moan and whispered, "What am I going to go? I think I'm going to throw up."

Logan grabbed his shoulders and shook him. "Look at me, damnit. You knew the risk. You'll be a gentleman and act accordingly because if you don't, I'll whip you within an inch of your life. Now smile like you mean it and go dance with her."

Wade wandered back to the austere woman and said something that made her smile, revealing pretty dimples. There appeared more to Mazie than a first glance revealed. The lamplight softened her angular features, making her more approachable. Logan prayed that Wade would do right by her.

The Widow Harvey smiled and stopped on her way to the punchbowl. "I'm sorry things didn't work out for us. I saw how badly Cali Rose wanted to win you."

Surprise rippled through Logan and he gave her a narrowed glance. "Mrs. Harvey, did you stop bidding on purpose?"

"Is that so hard to believe?" she asked softly.

Up close, he noticed barely a visible line yet she had to be around thirty. Or was that only something in his mind? It struck him that he didn't even know the littlest details about her. Had he cared so little? He shifted. The answer seemed obvious.

He was as bad as Wade at having preconceived notions about folks. Uncomfortable pricks ran up the back of his neck.

"At the risk of being too familiar, what is your first name, ma'am?"

"Jewel, and no I don't think you're being too forward."

"That's a pretty name. I like it, Jewel Harvey."

She met his eyes and he noticed hers were a rich dark brown that matched her hair. "You deserve to know why I participated in the auction." She raised her chin a trifle. "I thought I'd ask for your help with something. You look like the type of man a woman could depend on."

"I'll be happy to lend a hand with whatever you need, Mrs. ... Jewel. You have only to ask. Anytime."

"Very well." She adjusted the reticule on her arm. "My oldest son, Jeffrey, is breaking my heart, indulging in bad behavior, and speaking disrespectful. I wondered ...." she paused, tears filling her eyes. "I wondered if you'd speak to him. You're a fine, upstanding man, Logan Bartee, and I think he'd listen to you. He misses his father and needs a man to look up to."

Her high opinion startled him. He certainly wasn't any role model. He couldn't even keep Wade out of trouble.

Logan laid a comforting hand on her arm. "It's as good as done. I'll ride out to your place tomorrow morning and take Jeffrey fishing. That'll give us some privacy."

A smile lit up her face, making her eyes gleam like the color of rich, newly turned earth. "You're every bit the man I thought you were. Now go dance with Cali Rose."

Little she knew. He was nothing more than a bank robber and a fake. He just hadn't gotten caught is all. Yet somehow, that she thought him better than he was put a warmth in his chest.

"There you are, handsome." Cali Rose slipped her hand around his elbow.

"Yep. Waiting for you." Logan put an arm around her and swung her out into the center of the waltzing couples. The woman of his dreams was cozying up to him and all he could think about was his own shortcomings.

And the color of Jewel's eyes.

Tomorrow, he'd start on changing things and live up to the bargain he'd made with her.

* * *

The rooster had yet to crow and someone was pounding on his door. Logan jerked on his trousers and yelled, "Don't get your drawers in a wad!"

When he could force his eyes open, he was surprised to see Wade on his stoop. "You're up mighty early."

"You'll never believe what I have to tell you." The words left Wade so fast they almost formed a plume of steam. He didn't wait for an invite—just barged right past Logan.

"Don't let me stop you. Come right on in," he growled.

"What's the matter with you, grouchy butt?"

"I don't know, Wade. Maybe it has to do with being jarred out a sound sleep."

"It's time to get up. You can't lay in bed all day."

Truth be told, it was about last night. Cali Rose hadn't lived up to his expectations. She seemed shallow where Jewel Harvey showed a lot of gumption in picking up after her husband died and carrying on. That was one strong woman.

"Must need coffee." He stoked the fire on the stove, added a stick of wood, and slid the coffee he'd made yesterday on to heat. "Now what's so god-awful important?"

"Well, it's about Mazie."

Logan rubbed his face and sat on the bed to put his boots on. "What about her?"

"She's … well she's you know … a girl. I kissed her. Do you know who her brother is?" When Logan didn't say anything, Wade went on, "Her brother is the president of the bank, Todd Snodgrass."

"Okay." Damn, why couldn't Wade learn how to get to the point? He'd have to shave off a long white beard by the time Wade finished. "Just get on with it, for God's sake!"

"Mazie talked to her brother last night about my loan and Todd agreed to give me more time. Not only that, he wants me to work for him to pay off the loan. Can you believe that? I didn't get a wink of sleep for thinking about it." Wade glanced up from beneath the brim of his hat. "Logan, I think I'm in love."

"See how things work out when you least expect it? You were all in a panic when Mazie paid the winning bid for you. Remember that?"

"Why do you always have to bring up sour grapes? Huh?"

"Look, I just want you to learn from them. Want some coffee?"

"I wouldn't mind if I do."

Over the next hour, Logan told him about Jewel

Harvey and her request. "I could've crawled into a hole somewhere when she said I was a fine, upstanding man. I'm never going to get involved in your schemes again. Never."

"Well, you don't have to. I'm doing good on my own."

Logan gave Wade a grin. "Yes, it appears you are."

Working for the money instead of having it handed to him was just what Wade needed.

* * *

After breakfast, Logan saddled his horse and rode over to get Jeffrey Harvey. They located an excellent fishing spot and settled down on the bank.

Logan glanced at the boy who had yet to see his

first shave. "Your mother is worried about you, Jeffrey. Is something bothering you?"

"I miss my daddy. Why did he have to die and leave us?"

"I don't have that answer. Sorry. Some things no one can explain. I suppose it was his time."

Jeffrey met his gaze that was filled with pain. "Mama cries at night when she thinks we're all asleep. She works so hard trying to make ends meet—washing and ironing folks' clothes, taking care of their kids, selling eggs and butter. It's never enough."

Watching other folk's kids? Maybe all those he'd seen weren't hers.

"It's tough. How many brothers and sisters do you have?"

"It's just me and my little sister." Jeffrey skipped a rock across the water. "She's six."

They sat in silence for minute. Finally, Logan spoke in a quiet voice. "So why are you making things even harder for your mama? Doesn't she have enough to worry about?"

"I'm scared, Mr. Bartee. Real scared. If she dies, what will me and my sister do? We'd have to go to an orphanage."

"That won't happen as long I'm alive," Logan said, his voice gruff. He thought a minute. "If I can find you a job, you'd be helping."

Jeffrey's head whipped around, hope on his face. "Do you think anyone would hire me?"

"Sure. I noticed a sign yesterday in the general store wanting help. You could sweep the floors and tote boxes. When we get tired of fishing, we'll head into town. I'll talk to old man Jenkins for you but I'm sure he'll hire you on the spot."

"Thanks, Mr. Bartee. I feel a lot better now."

Logan draped an arm across the kid's skinny shoulders. "Good. Come talk to me when you start letting anger and despair roll over you. Deal?"

"Deal." Jeffrey's grin stretched across his face.

The kid just needed someone with a listening ear. Maybe that was all anyone needed. He thought of Jewel. When he took Jeffrey home, if she asked him to come in he would.

Hard luck wouldn't follow anyone who was willing to look beyond the surface. Now that he thought on it, Jewel couldn't be a bit older than his twenty-eight. Why he remembered his mother saying that Jewel had married at sixteen. She wasn't old at all.

A chuckle broke the silence. He'd worn blinders his whole life. But no more.

LETTER TO THE READER

Sometimes stories come to me in novel form and other times they're short and simple but hopefully with a powerful message. I never know what I'm going to do with the shorter ones but I write them and trust God to put them in the right hands. Each story here reveals the hopes and dreams of people who have little else. They share a kinship with those settlers who came West looking for a better life. Some are missing pieces of themselves and needing something to fill the hole in their heart. All are lonely and at times want to give up and quit. But they don't. Something deep inside prods them to keep living and trying.

I think I have much of the pioneer spirit inside me. So many times life has knocked me to my knees but I got up. Maybe I'm just stubborn. I really don't see myself as having exceptional courage. I've been homeless twice in my life and it's nothing I want to repeat again.

For the first years of my life, I lived in a tent with my parents and three siblings. No running water. No bathroom. No space to wiggle. We were long on poverty and short on hope. But, my parents who went through the Depression didn't quit either so maybe that's where this almighty stubbornness comes from.

In 1998, I was diagnosed with multiple sclerosis and life took another huge turn and I had to reach deep inside and find strength I didn't know I had. It was about that time I published my first book and I remember how excited I was to have reached the dream that I'd carried so long. It was like life gave me good to offset the bad. But I've never complained. I don't have that right. There are lots of others who have worse things. I've always been taught to take the hand you're given and make the best of the situation. All in all, I've been immensely blessed.

My brother told me that MS stands for Mighty Spirit. I don't know about that, but I like to think it does. Maybe you have Mighty Spirit too.

I pray you enjoy these stories and maybe they'll bring a laugh or find a place in your heart. You can contact me through my website LindaBroday.com. I'm also on Facebook, Twitter, Goodreads, BookBub and other places. Write me. I love to hear from readers!

ABOUT LINDA

I'm a *New York Times* and *USA Today* bestselling author of full-length historical western romance novels and novellas.

I set all my stories in Texas because the history and people of this state runs bone-deep. This land is old and stained with blood of those who wanted to live free. I live in the panhandle on land the American Indian and Comancheros once roamed and I can often hear their voices whispering in the wind.

Watching TV westerns during my youth fed my love of cowboys and the old West and they still do. I'm inspired to tell stories of the heroism and courage of these valiant men who ride the range. As Willie Nelson says in his song "My Heroes Have Always Been Cowboys": *Sadly, in search of, but one step in back of themselves and their slow movin' dreams.*

Next to writing, I love research and looking for little tidbits to add realism to my stories. I've been accused (and quite unfairly I might add) of making a nuisance of myself at museums, libraries, and historical places. I'm also a movie buff and love sitting in a dark theater, watching the magic on the screen. As long as I'm confessing…chocolate is my best friend. It just soothes my soul.

Contact Links:

Visit me at: www.LindaBroday.com

Facebook Author Page:
http://www.facebook.com/lindabrodayauthor

On Twitter: http://twitter.com/lbroday

Amazon Author Page: http://www.amazon.com/Linda-Broday/e/B001JRXWB2

Goodreads: https://www.goodreads.com/author/show/1204489.Linda_Broday

Pinterest: http://www.pinterest.com/lindabroday1/

BookBub: https://www.bookbub.com/authors/linda-broday

CPSIA information can be obtained
at www.ICGtesting.com
Printed in the USA
BVHW04s1821230818
525444BV00009B/129/P